"Amy, you know this is madness."

But even as Matt spoke, his strong, lean hands were sliding hungrily over her body, caressing her with tender persuasion.

Swinging her into his arms, he carried her out of the studio and up the stairs. He held her effortlessly, and she wound her slim arms around his neck, pressing soft kisses against his face as they moved.

He laid her on his bed gently; then he was beside her, reaching for her, the need undisguised in his face and his hands.

"I love you, Matt," Amy whispered, unable to stop the words from forming on her lips. And someday soon she would be unable to stop the pain of having loved Matt Cavanagh—the pain of having lost him completely.

WELCOME
TO THE WONDERFUL WORLD
OF *Harlequin Presents*

Interesting, informative and entertaining,
each Harlequin romance portrays an appealing
and original love story. With a varied array
of settings, we may lure you on an African safari,
to a quaint Welsh village, or an exotic Riviera
location—anywhere and everywhere that adventurous
men and women fall in love.

As publishers of Harlequin romances, we're
extremely proud of our books. Since 1949,
Harlequin Enterprises has built its publishing
reputation on the solid base of quality and
originality. Our stories are the most popular
paperback romances sold in North America; every
month, six new titles are released and sold at
nearly every book-selling store in Canada and the
United States.

A free catalogue listing all available Harlequin romances
can be yours by writing to the

HARLEQUIN READER SERVICE
1440 South Priest Drive, Tempe, AZ 85281
Canadian address: Stratford, Ontario N5A 6W2

We sincerely hope you enjoy reading
this Harlequin Presents.

Yours truly,

THE PUBLISHERS

PATRICIA LAKE

untamed witch

Harlequin Books

TORONTO • LONDON • LOS ANGELES • AMSTERDAM
SYDNEY • HAMBURG • PARIS • STOCKHOLM • ATHENS • TOKYO

Harlequin Presents edition published November 1981
ISBN 0-373-10465-0

Original hardcover edition published in 1981
by Mills & Boon Limited

CHAPTER ONE

AMY LAWRENCE stepped out into the bright summer sunshine, pulling closed the exotically painted poppy-red door behind her. Walking briskly down the path, she breathed in deeply, enjoying the warm balmy air and the sweet scent of the wild garden.

She had loved this garden for as long as she could remember. As a small child, she had visited her grandparents often, spending long golden days lying in the emerald grass, watching with a child's wonder the amazing variety of busy life, never still and always changing, that bustled quietly there all summer long. Smiling gently at herself as that wide-eyed little girl, Amy made her way down to the village, a large wicker basket slung carelessly over her arm. Strolling along the narrow lane, she realised how happy she was, living with her grandfather; everything was so peaceful here, and her days were calm and uncomplicated. Never again would she complicate her life, she thought fiercely, flicking a strand of heavy black hair over her shoulder and turning the corner that brought her on to the main street of the quiet village.

An hour, and some pleasant gossip later, with the rest of her shopping done, she was walking into the chemist to pick up a prescription for her grandfather before returning home, when she was suddenly confronted by a tall, powerful man blocking her entrance. As she glanced up at him with a murmured apology, Amy's heart suddenly stopped, air seemed locked in her lungs, and she could not breathe. For

long seconds she stared up into his face, until he
broke the silence by saying quietly, 'Hello, Amy, how
have you been?'

'Matt . . .?' she whispered incredulously, totally
unaware of the curious glances they were both re-
ceiving from other customers in the shop. Amy could
feel herself trembling, her thoughts totally chaotic as
Matt's darkly enigmatic eyes slowly appraised her
slender body thoroughly, making her instantly aware
of her shabby sky-blue cotton dress and bare brown
legs.

His eyes narrowed piercingly, as they returned to
her face, and sensing some unspoken criticism, Amy
lifted her head and thrust forward her delicate chin,
flicking him what she hoped was a cold, disdainful
glance. Don't be so stupid, she admonished herself
sternly; Matt Cavanagh means nothing to you after
all these years. Nothing, so don't give him the satisfaction of seeing any weakness in you.

So, summoning the last ounces of her willpower,
she forced herself not to run down the street, away
from him, like a frightened child, and looking coolly
into his eyes, she said quietly, 'I'm fine, thank you.
And how are you?'

Matt's eyes mocked her strained voice, and her
nervous fingers playing with the basket. He did not
reply for what seemed to Amy's screaming nerves
long silent moments. Instead, he guided her away
from the shop doorway, his long hard-skinned fingers
sending shivers of fire through the elbow they
grasped. Even as her heart beat wildly at his touch,
Amy's thoughts were angry. That they should meet
by chance after all these years seemed unbelievable,
and she felt frightened and suspicious. 'What are you
doing here?' The words were blurted out defiantly,
her hard-worn coolness forgotten in the tumult of

conflicting emotions that besieged her confused mind. 'How did you find me?'

The gentle mockery left Matt's eyes, and they hardened angrily at her furious questions, making her cringe inwardly, remembering his ruthless cruelty when angry. Then the anger was gone, maybe she had imagined it, and a blank shuttered look closed his face to her searching eyes. 'Whatever I'm doing here, my love, you can rest assured that it has absolutely nothing to do with you,' he drawled slowly, lighting a cigarette with practised ease, and inhaling the smoke deep into his lungs. Amy watched his movements abstractedly, realising sadly that she had never forgotten his smooth, feline grace. No man she had ever met moved like Matt Cavanagh.

The fact that she had forgotten nothing about him in the last three years angered her further. Damn him for coming here! She would never forgive him for upsetting her so deeply again, just when she thought she had cleansed her mind and treacherous body of longing for him. Her angry thoughts were interrupted by his movement catching her eye, as he flexed his powerful shoulder muscles, stretching the thin denim material of his shirt tautly across the smooth skin she had known so intimately. This disturbing thought was more than Amy could cope with, and uttering a smothered cry, she turned and ran like the wind down the street, needing to get away from him, uncaring of the strange looks people were giving her, and knowing that his dark eyes followed her every inch of the way.

She ran till her lungs were bursting, and even then did not stop until she reached home. It was only then she remembered her grandfather's prescription.

She unpacked and stored away her shopping with

trembling hands, then sat down with a cup of coffee and a much-needed cigarette. She could not find her purse and supposed she had dropped it in her flight from the village, but somehow she did not really care. Thoughts of Matt Cavanagh, and his appearance in the village, made it unimportant.

Someone will pick it up and give it back when they see me, she thought dully, although she felt like never going down to the village again. As she smoked and drank her coffee, she forced herself to gather her scattered wits and think sensibly. It was more than likely that Matt was just passing through—after all, there was nothing for him here. She probably would not see him again. Feeling this to be logical, Amy felt somewhat calmer as she drained her coffee cup. Glancing at the clock, she was shocked to see that it was almost lunchtime. Her five-minute encounter with Matt Cavanagh had wasted her whole morning, and she firmly put him out of her mind and began preparing lunch for her grandfather and herself.

She was just placing plates of deliciously roasted cold chicken and crisp salad on the table when her grandfather came in.

'Just on time, as usual, Granddad,' she smiled, kissing his cheek affectionately.

He grinned wryly. 'The one thing your grandmother insisted on, Amy love, was everyone being on time for meals, God rest her soul. I reckon I just got into the habit.' His face sobered as he thought of his wife. Charlotte Lawrence had died of pneumonia eight years before, leaving her husband bereft, after forty years of companionable marriage. Amy had brought sunshine back into his life, and he loved her dearly. That was why he hesitated in telling her the news he had heard in the village that morning.

When she had first come to Cornwall to live with

him, he knew she had been badly hurt. The haunted paleness of her face and the quietly desperate moods that lasted for days at a time, told him without words. He was the only person she had to turn to, her parents having been killed in a road accident, one foggy winter's night when Amy was only four. He had also known the cause of her deep sadness, and now—ah, well, she had to be told.

'Er . . . Amy——' he began, clearing his throat, 'I was talking to Seth Greenwood today, in the village. He was saying that Matt Cavanagh has rented Old Farm Cottage for the summer. . . .' Amy's fork clattered noisily on to the table, her face suddenly white. 'I'm sorry, lass, but I thought you ought to know— with you and him. . . .' His voice trailed off at the look on his granddaughter's face. He wished he could have spared her this news. Cavanagh had caused enough trouble already, and he felt angry.

'It's . . . it's okay, Granddad,' Amy replied stiffly 'Actually I . . . er . . . I . . . met him today in the village. He doesn't change, I'd have recognised him anywhere.' She tried to laugh lightly, without much success. 'Anyway, don't you worry, I got over him years ago, I wouldn't care if he was living next door.' She got up quickly, and cleared the plates from the table, taking them into the kitchen to make coffee. Once in the kitchen, she leaned back against the door, pressing a trembling hand to her forehead. Oh, God! He had rented the cottage for the summer. That meant he would be here in the village for at least three months.

So much for her thoughts of never seeing him again, she thought, a trifle hysterically. She would see him all over the place, and she knew she could not stand it. Perhaps she could go away. But no, she squashed that idea quickly, realising that if she was

ever going to get over Matt Cavanagh, running away
would not help. She had to stay and face him, if
necessary, to show him that he meant nothing to
her. Whether or not that was true, Amy did not
allow herself to think about, but she knew that she
had made a complete fool of herself in front of him,
in the village, and she vowed that it would not
happen again.

Given new strength by her positive thoughts, she
quickly made the coffee and carrying it into the
dining room, found that she could chat quite calmly
for the rest of the meal.

Later that afternoon, when her grandfather had
gone to help Seth Greenwood on his allotment, Amy
was arranging sweet-smelling roses in one of her
grandmother's beautiful crystal vases, when there
was a knock on the door. It was a loud authoritative
rap, and her heart began to race as she smoothed
down her wild black hair and moved to open the
door. The sight of Matt Cavanagh leaning indolently
against the door jamb took her breath away. He did
not waste any time, she thought warily.

'Can I come in?' he asked mockingly, as she stood,
totally still, staring at him. Probably with her mouth
open, she realised shamefully. Flushing delicately
under his lazy scrutiny, she held open the door. 'If
you must!' she muttered ungraciously; knowing him
as she did, she knew that if he wanted to come in he
would—invited or not.

'You're too kind, lovely Amy,' he murmured
softly. 'Although I can see that your manners haven't
improved in all these years.'

He strolled past her into the small cottage, and
watching him covertly from under her lashes, she
treated him to the same thorough inspection he had
given her that morning. He had not changed much

in three years. He was a tall, powerfully built man, yet there was not an ounce of spare flesh on his muscular frame. The denim shirt he was wearing exposed the strong brown column of his throat, and the beginnings of the thick black hair that matted his broad chest. Faded denim jeans hugged his lean hips and flat stomach tightly, moulding his strong muscular thighs. He moved with a light, panther-like grace that belied his powerful body. Her gaze moved upwards. His hair was thick and black, and she painfully remembered the feel of its crisp vitality under her fingers. His eyes were dark and unfathomable, under thick, dark brows, his cheekbones were hard and pronounced, making his face seem all planes and smooth powerful angles. His nose was straight, and his mouth hard and sensual. The passage of three years was apparent only in the deep, cynical lines that slashed his face. He exuded an amazing sexual magnetism that, even now, made Amy's pulses leap.

He caught her staring at him, and returned her look with one of lazy, sardonic amusement. She immediately looked away, hot colour staining her cheeks.

'Aren't you going to offer me a drink?' he enquired smoothly, amusement still apparent in his face.

'No,' she replied shortly. 'Tell me what you've come for and then go. I don't want you near me, now or ever again!' She knew she had gone too far when his eyes narrowed darkly, and he strode over to her, gripping her shoulders with both hands, his strong fingers digging into her soft flesh, making her catch her breath.

'Don't try my patience, Amy,' he grated harshly, shaking her slightly and making her wince with discomfort.

'Let me go, you cruel swine, you're hurting me!' she shouted with sudden ridiculous tears threatening to overflow down her face. 'I hate you, Matt Cavanagh! Your touch insults me. . . .' She got no further. His mouth came down on hers suddenly and cruelly, his lips punishing, as he released his grip on her shoulders and pulled her into his arms. She struggled violently, twisting futilely within the steel-strong circle of his embrace. She kept her lips tightly closed under the sweet, demanding pressure of his, but her actions only served to deepen his insistent desire, and God help her, she could feel herself responding. How could it be like this after three years apart? she asked herself wearily, desperately.

He lifted his head, and the dark, arousing fever in his eyes made her bones melt, and she knew that nothing mattered except being in his arms.

'Amy,' he murmured unsteadily, 'it's been too long.' He lowered his head, and his hard mouth explored her face gently, as his hands were sliding over her body possessively, knowing with the ease of a lover how to arouse and excite her. She could feel the heat rising within her. She could no longer resist him. Indeed, she did not want to. Her lips parted beneath his, and she heard with a pounding heart his muffled groan, as he plundered the long-denied sweetness of her mouth, with a hunger that made her cling to him.

His strong arms tightened around her, straining her even closer, and with a moan of pure need, the need that she had stifled for three lonely years, she slid her arms around his neck, arching her soft body in total surrender against the hard length of him. He lifted his head almost immediately, his eyes half-closed, glazed with desire, and she looked into his face uncertainly, sensing his withdrawal, just in time to see the blank, unfathomable look she was used to, shutter his eyes, giving his face the look of a taut mask.

His mouth twisted viciously. 'It didn't take long, did it, Amy?' His tone was sneering and contemptuous. 'So you can't stand me near you, my touch insults you—I wouldn't have said that ten seconds ago, would you?'

She turned away blindly, unwilling to show him the shame and humiliation that was cutting into her, at his cruel jibes. She wanted to cry, but she knew she was past that relief. And the worst thing of all was that even now, after his calculated and deliberate insults, if he pulled her into his arms she still wanted him, and would respond fully and passionately.

She could hear him moving, and turned towards him, not meeting his eyes, for fear of what she might see in them. He was standing by the door. Lying in his open hand was her purse.

'You dropped it this morning,' he said quietly, his tone guarded. He placed it on the table and walked out of the cottage.

Amy sank into the nearest chair, trembling reaction shaking her body. She buried her head in her hands, totally weary and utterly defeated. She sat like that for several hours, her mind numb, her body still aching for the fulfilment only Matt Cavanagh could provide. Finally, realising that her grandfather would soon be in for dinner, she forced herself to move from the chair and prepare the evening meal. She felt dazed as her hands mechanically made pastry, and peeled and washed vegetables. Unable to help herself, she was still in the same trance-like state throughout dinner. She pushed her food around the plate, miserably, unable to manage more than a few choking mouthfuls of the delicious meal, that tasted to her of sawdust and ashes. Her grandfather noticed her silence, her bleak, haunted eyes, and wisely said nothing. After a few abortive attempts at conversation which Amy did not appear to hear, he reached for his newspaper and buried his head behind it.

After clearing the table and washing the dishes, Amy decided to take a shower. Perhaps it would wash away Matt's touch, and make her feel normal again. Stripping off the blue dress quickly, she plunged under the icy needles of the shower. Turning the taps full on, she gasped as the cold water pelted her overheated body. She scrubbed herself vigorously, until her skin tingled, and it seemed to work. At least she felt alive again, even if she could not lift the deep depression that covered her thoughts like a thick blanket of grey fog.

Stepping out of the shower, she wrapped herself in a thick, fluffy towel and rubbed herself dry. Standing before the mirror, she let the towel drop, and examined her body curiously. Her skin was golden, and had a pearly sheen to it. She was a tall, slender girl, although she had always thought her breasts too prominent for her to look really elegant. Her legs were long and slim, her hips curving sensuously above them, up to her slight waist and flat stomach. As she ran her hands slowly over her body, she could not deny that she was a woman, with a woman's needs. Matt Cavanagh had been her lover three long years ago. Her first and only lover. He had possessed and fulfilled her, teaching her love, and desire, and need. And she had suppressed all these things until today, when in his arms, all her half-buried emotions had risen to the surface and overwhelmed her.

Damn him, she thought for at least the tenth time that day, turning her attention to her face. Her thick and shiny black hair hung long and wild, almost to her waist. She remembered with an aching heart Matt brushing it out with gentle hands, burying his face in the scented darkness of it, wrapping it around his neck to pull her closer. Impatiently she pulled a comb through the tangled locks, uncaring of the pain to her tender scalp.

Her face was pointed, her features delicate, with the exception of her eyes. Huge and topaz, fringed with thick black lashes, they usually carried a gentle and serene expression. Her mouth was soft and vulnerable, hiding perfect white teeth. She was totally unaware of her striking beauty, and the calm gentleness that people who met her hardly ever forgot.

Sighing, she dried her hair, plaiting it in one thick pigtail down her back, and slipped on a thin silk robe in black, scattered with embroidered flowers. She felt miserable and lonely, and there was no point in denying it to herself any longer. She loved Matt Cavanagh, despite everything he had done. She always would.

Making some coffee, and lighting a cigarette, she sat back in an easy chair, and for the first time in years allowed herself to think back on her affair with Matt. . . .

CHAPTER TWO

Amy had been brought up by her aunt, her mother's sister, after her parents had been killed. She could hardly remember her parents, and Juliet, her aunt, had made sure that her little niece lacked for nothing. When she went to live in their large, noisy and affectionate house they considered her their own daughter, and she remembered her childhood as bright, sunny and filled with laughter.

At the age of seventeen, when her aunt and uncle moved to West Germany, she had just left school. Her uncle had been offered a highly-paid engineering job there and, not wanting to leave the country, Amy and her cousin Joni, who was more like a sister, took a flat together in London. The flat was large and elegant, in a rambling Victorian house in Kensington, and the girls both looked for jobs as soon as they moved in. Joni, who was small, blonde and cheerful, found a job almost immediately at the Victoria and Albert Museum, which she loved, although Amy suspected that it was Joni's bubbling personality and easy ability to make friends that made the job so enjoyable. Amy herself, who had always loved painting, perhaps because her father had been an artist, found a job as general dogsbody at a small gallery in the West End. She worked hard, typing, answering the phone and helping to set up the exhibitions, and within a year had become indispensable to John Wilson, the gallery owner. She became his personal assistant, a little surprised at the promotion, but very pleased, because she was

16

fond of John, seeing him almost as a father figure. She was unaware that he found her utterly enchanting, never noticing how his attitude would harden protectively when he caught men staring at the beautiful grace and innocence that was Amy. For her part, she ignored most of them. She was only eighteen, and a little unsure of herself with men, especially the hard, sophisticated types that tended to patronise the gallery.

She remembered clearly John walking into the gallery one morning, his face wreathed with smiles, and excitement in his voice, as he told her, 'We're going to be showing Matthew Cavanagh's work next month!' Amy had heard of Matthew Cavanagh, of course, he was already a well-known and much admired sculptor. She had seen one or two pieces of his work, and was fascinated by them. She had also seen photographs of him in the newspapers, never smiling, his hard face always grim. Still, John was looking well pleased with himself, and she was glad for his sake. The gallery did need something like this to give it a boost.

John informed her that Cavanagh was calling in later that afternoon, advising her to cancel any other appointments.

'Do be nice to him, Amy,' he had said. 'He's the biggest artist we've had and we don't want to lose him. I hear he's a bit of a temperamental chap, so let's all jump to attention.' Amy had laughed at this, but had promised to do her best.

At two o'clock precisely that afternoon, Matthew Cavanagh had walked into the gallery, and into Amy's life. She had just got back from a rushed lunch with Joni, looking in vain for a pair of shoes in the same outrageous shade of red as a dress that Joni had bought the week before. Joni always seemed to have problems finding colour matches, because as Amy laughingly told her, she always bought the brightest and most daring clothes she could find.

Amy herself was wearing a pale yellow cotton dress, loose-fitting, but hinting at the curved figure beneath. She looked very lovely with her midnight hair cascading down her back, and the dress reflecting the gold of her eyes, and Matt Cavanagh's breath was taken away by her when he walked into the gallery.

She was, he thought, mocking his own sentimentality, the woman he had never found during the past thirty years of his life, and he wanted her.

Amy stood up and smiled her bright, serene smile as he reached her desk. 'Mr Cavanagh? Mr Wilson will see you immediately, if you'll come this way.' Her head dropped suddenly, delicate colour staining her cheeks, and he realised that he had been staring at her, and she was embarrassed. That in itself was unusual in most of the women he had known, and he was intrigued. He tilted up her chin gently with his thumb.

'Your name?' he asked quietly.

'Amy—Amy Lawrence,' she answered, and smiled at him, her embarrassment gone. Wearing a close-fitting dark blue pin-striped suit, and a white shirt, he looked strong, hard and very masculine. She felt drawn to him.

'Have dinner with me tonight, Amy,' he commanded softly, his dark eyes gentle, as they rested on her upturned face.

'Well—er . . . that is . . .' she stumbled over her words, but she could not deny that she wanted to go with him, so why not. 'Yes, please, Mr Cavanagh,' she replied.

'Matt,' he said firmly, still holding her chin.

'Matt,' she repeated obediently, and he smiled. Amy was devastated, and her heart began to race. He was, without doubt, the most attractive, magnetic man she had ever seen.

At that moment John Wilson came out of his office, a concerned look on his face. 'Amy isn't . . .?' he began, and then spotted Matt standing just in front of her. He introduced himself, and they shook hands, Matt acknowledging the introduction with a polite nod. John turned as they reached his office. 'Amy, take notes, will you?'

Nodding, Amy grabbed her pad and pen and followed them in. This initial meeting went well, and she could see that John was well pleased as Matt outlined briefly and succinctly what he wanted. Her pen flew over her notebook, and she was aware of Matt's dark eyes on her the whole time.

The meeting over, she returned to her desk. On his way out of the gallery Matt leaned over her desk and said.

'I'll pick you up at eight. Give me your address.'

Wondering if she hadn't been a bit hasty, she gave him her address and he left. She felt nervous when he had gone. Never before had she accepted an invitation to dinner from a virtual stranger, and she wondered if she should cancel. She was still musing on this, a frown creasing her smooth brow, when a boy entered the gallery with an armful of sweet peas, bursting with colour and scent.

'Miss Lawrence?' She nodded, speechless. Nobody had ever sent her flowers before. She opened the card with eager hands after thanking the boy. The message read simply, They remind me of you—Matt. The strong black writing reminded her of him, and she shivered involuntarily, knowing that he would be ruthless in pursuit of what he wanted. But surely

that was not her. She bent her head to the soft
flowers. They smelled so beautiful, so fresh, in the
dry dusty heat of a London afternoon.

Joni was envious and astonished when Amy told
her of the dinner date. 'You lucky devil! Matt
Cavanagh, he's really something.' Her eyes were
dreamy as she spoke. 'Where are you going?'

'I don't know, somewhere frightfully expensive, I
suppose,' replied Amy absently, wondering whether
or not to wear her hair up. She knew that it made
her look older, and she did not want Matt Cavanagh
guessing that she was only eighteen. In the end she
settled for a sophisticated chignon that emphasised
her delicate bone structure and long graceful neck.

She had decided to wear a golden Indian print
dress that she had bought a month previously, for a
party. It was subtly patterned and the tight bodice
was a bright patchwork of velvet, satin and beads.
Together with high-heeled sandals and a light make-
up she knew that she was looking her best.

At eight o'clock sharp when the bell rang Amy's
stomach turned over sharply, making her feel sick.
Trying to appear cool but in fact feeling incredibly
nervous, she opened the front door and peered out.
Matt stood on the step and she suddenly felt very
young and naïve as she stared at him. He was
wearing a dark evening jacket that accentuated the
powerful width of his shoulders, and the darkness of
his eyes. He smiled at her gently, aware of her nervousness. 'You look very beautiful, Amy,' he said
sincerely, putting her at ease. 'Shall we go?'

As she slid into his low, powerful car, a sense of
reckless excitement filled her. Beneath his formal
exterior she recognised Matt's wild, primitive magnetism. She could see it in his eyes when he looked
at her, and she was suddenly so very glad that she

had accepted his dinner invitation. She wanted to know him, and gazing at his hard mouth covertly, as he drove, she wondered what it would be like to be kissed by him. She felt sure that it would be a unique experience, and flushed at her thoughts.

He caught the flush on her face as he glanced at her. 'What were you thinking just now?' he asked lazily, his voice low and indulgent.

'What it would be like to be kissed by you.' Horrified, Amy heard her own honest reply. She cursed her own childishness. Good heavens, what would he think of her? The car slid to a halt and Matt's arm came around her shoulders. She could feel the hard muscles flexing easily behind her neck, and turned towards him intending to apologise. She never got the chance. His hard mouth brushed hers slowly, and she quivered at his touch, hearing his low growl of laughter as he lifted his head. 'Don't tempt me, Amy,' he murmured, amusement in his face as she stared at him, wide-eyed. Kissing her forehead gently, he started the engine, and pulled back on to the road.

The restaurant, as Amy suspected, was expensive and richly exclusive. They talked and laughed together while eating the beautifully prepared food. Skilfully Matt drew her out, and she talked unselfconsciously about herself. He was charming and witty, and his eyes darkened disturbingly as he watched her.

Amy felt proud and elated to be with him. He was unlike anyone she had met before. She could see a number of women in the restaurant eyeing Matt openly, although he seemed unaware of their pointed glances. He made her feel beautiful and important, and she could feel herself falling under his fascinating spell.

Leaving the restaurant some hours later, Amy felt more than a little lightheaded. She had drunk rather a lot of wine in an effort to lose her inhibiting nervousness, and as she slid into the comfortable car she flashed Matt a dazzling smile, her golden eyes too brilliant in her flushed face.

'It was a lovely meal, Matt, really lovely, thank you.'

'I'd better take you home,' he laughed softly.

'I'd like to go to the sea, and wade, watch the moon, and sit on the sand,' Amy said dreamily, her eyes huge and far-away.

'Well, if that's what you want, lady, that's what you shall have.' His smile was indulgent as he deftly manoeuvred the car into the busy traffic. Feeling incredibly wide awake, Amy watched the twinkling lights in the distance as they drove, and sighed happily. She wanted this evening to last for ever, and she was more than a little in love with Matt Cavanagh already. She glanced at his hands on the steering wheel. They were strong and long-fingered, and she quivered inwardly, imagining them on her body. Her instinct told her that he knew a great deal about women, and she experienced her first pangs of jealousy, wondering how many lovers he had known.

She was still wrestling with these hitherto unknown emotions when the car slid quietly to a standstill. She looked up quickly. They were parked on the edge of a lonely stretch of sand. A few hundred yards in front of them was the sea, glinting silver in the light of the almost full moon.

Amy sat for long moments spellbound at the beauty of the scene before her.

'Come on, let's walk,' said Matt, breaking the silence, as he shrugged off his jacket and pulled off his tie.

She got out of the car and kicked off her sandals, enjoying the feel of the cool powdery sand beneath her toes. She gulped in huge breaths of salt-filled air, clearing her head, and giggling like a child.

Matt watched her, an expression that she could not recognise in his dark eyes.

'Come here,' he ordered softly, and she walked towards him and stood looking up into his face, smiling.

His hands deftly removed the pins from her hair, and it fell loose and soft down her back. He threaded his fingers through it, marvelling at the soft warmth that it left in his hands.

'Always wear it this way for me.' His voice was deep and strangely harsh, and feeling a little frightened of the turmoil that his voice awakened in her, Amy turned on her heel and ran towards the sea. Matt stood watching her intently, her long graceful legs and wild hair, the beauty of her movement, for long seconds before following her. When he caught up to her she was paddling, holding her dress above the water, and gasping at the cold shock to her legs and feet. She urged him into the water with her, and they splashed like children under the velvet twinkling sky.

Later, they lay on their backs in the sand, and Matt taught Amy about the stars. She wished on the first falling star that she saw, that he could perhaps be feeling the way she was. Laughing, she filled his trouser pockets with shells, and tiny slivers of coral, and neither of them noticed the dark night slipping away. They walked together along the edge of the water, hand in hand, a strange and silent contentment between them, until Amy spotted an old tree, growing by itself, sticking out of the sand like a monument.

'I think that tree must be magic, growing like that,' she said, and pulling her hand out of his, walked over to it. She stretched her arms around the trunk, laying her cheek against the rough bark. Matt followed, and placing a hand on either side of her, effectively trapped her.

'I think it's you who has the magic,' he said smilingly. 'You can make me feel like a boy again, looking at the world through a child's eyes. You're a witch, Amy, a beautiful, untamed witch.' The smile died in his eyes, as his glance slid to her mouth, her lips parted and vulnerable.

She felt dizzy as his mouth descended, brushing hers sensuously. She lifted her hands to his shoulders to steady herself, feeling the powerful muscles tighten beneath her fingers. His kiss deepened, as her breathing quickened. 'Open your mouth,' he ordered, his breath hot against her lips. She obeyed immediately, and he pulled her against his body. Desire flared up inside her, his touch made her feel fiery, and she had an ache in the pit of her stomach that she knew he could assuage.

'Matt . . .' she whispered achingly, as his mouth trailed fire to her throat, making her tremble, and arch her body against his. She heard his swift intake of breath as she moved against him, and then his mouth returned to hers, hard, demanding and devastatingly male, in its possession. She responded instinctively to him, wanting to satisfy him, but suddenly he thrust her away from him, putting a few yards between them and standing with his back turned.

Any felt bereft and confused at this sudden rejection. 'Matt?' she whispered sadly. 'Did I do something wrong?' Matt did not answer, but ran his hand around the back of his neck, flexing his shoulder muscles wearily. 'Matt?'

'No, Amy,' he finally answered, his voice harsh and barely controlled. 'You did nothing wrong.'

'Don't you want me?' this, hardly audible in her fear of total rejection. He heard the pain and confusion in her voice, and spun to face her angrily.

'Dammit, Amy, of course I want you! You're beautiful. But I'm not in the habit of seducing young, inexperienced virgins!'

She stood stricken, her eyes wide with hurt, as his anger lashed over her. Turning wordlessly, she ran back towards the car, tears that she could not control pouring down her face.

She heard him calling her, somewhere behind, but ignored him, running blindly on. It was true that she was inexperienced, but that was hardly her fault, she thought miserably.

He caught up with her effortlessly, grasping her shoulders and turning her to face him. His glance took in her tear-stained face and hurt eyes, and he felt an utter swine for crushing her so completely, so needlessly.

'Amy, Amy, don't cry,' he groaned, folding his strong arms around her, comforting her.

'I'm sorry,' she sniffed despairingly.

'I didn't mean to hurt you, believe me. You're so young and beautiful. I couldn't take that innocence from you, however much I want to.' He wiped away her tears with gentle fingers, and she felt calmer, and happier, knowing that his words had not been calculated to hurt.

'I'm sorry, Matt,' she whispered softly, needing to say something. 'I suppose I'm just tired, and overreacting. I didn't mean to be so stupid,' she smiled at him.

'You're not stupid,' he smiled back at her, and

understanding each other, they strolled, hand in hand, back to the car.

Both were silent during the journey home. Amy's thoughts were filled with her new awareness of her own body. Men had kissed her before, but none of them had made her feel the way Matt could. She glanced at his strong, clear profile, knowing that he too was thinking about the incident on the beach, and cursed her youth and inexperience.

Matt had wanted her as they had stood locked together on that deserted beach. His passion had been barely controlled, and the memory of the molten desire she had glimpsed in his eyes made her feel weak, even now. She sighed wearily. He probably would not want to see her again.

Her thoughts were interrupted by his voice as the car slid noiselessly to a standstill in front of her flat. She shook herself out of her reverie, surprised that they were back in London so soon.

'I beg your pardon?' she said, turning to look at him, her expression blank.

'I want you to sit for me,' he repeated slowly.

'Me?' she echoed, unable to take this in.

'Yes, you, Amy. I'll pick you up at noon on Sunday. Right?' An indulgent smile curved his hard mouth, but his eyes were intent and serious, on her tired and confused face.

'Right,' she replied, shaking her head. A little bubble of happiness exploded inside her at the thought of seeing him again. She fumbled for the door handle, feeling absurdly happy. 'I can't open the door,' she smiled. Shaking his head with amusement, he leaned over, his arm brushing the softness of her breasts, and flicked open the door. Pressing her lips to his smooth, hard cheek, surprised at her own daring, she slipped out of the car and ran to the front door. Finding her key, she entered to the sound of the car's purring engine as it drew away. She danced into the flat, her face sobering as she noticed the time. Four-thirty. Oh well, it was Saturday tomorrow—today. Stuck on the kitchen door, in a prominent position, was a note from Joni. It read:—

I waited up for as long as I could. What have you been up to? I expect a full report tomorrow, you lucky thing! J.

Amy giggled, imagining Joni waiting up for her, bursting with curiosity, until her eyes closed and she had to give up. Creeping around the flat, she washed and undressed, and only when she was beneath the covers did she allow herself to re-live the evening. She drifted into a deep, contented sleep with Matt's face, his eyes dark and lazy, imprinted on her mind, and filling her dreams.

She was wakened at eleven the next morning by Joni, carrying a cup of coffee and with a curious expression.

'Good heavens, Amy!' she exclaimed. 'How long are you going to sleep? I can't contain my curiosity any longer, so you'll have to get up!' Amy pulled herself into a sitting position and yawned loudly.

Joni eyed her intently. 'What time did you get in?' she questioned suspiciously.

'Four-thirty, if you must know,' replied Amy, still yawning.

'Four-thirty?' Joni echoed. 'What on earth were you doing until that late?' she giggled, 'or perhaps I shouldn't ask!'

Amy raised her eyebrows. 'We drove to a beach, and paddled and watched the stars,' she replied dreamily.

'You and Matt Cavanagh?' Joni was obviously

having difficulty believing her.

'Yes. He's quite human, you know.'

'You don't have to tell me!' groaned Joni. 'Those sexy eyes, that body and his low, come-to-bed voice. . . .'

'Can I smell burning?' asked Amy innocently.

'Damn—the toast!' Joni ran from the room, cursing in an unladylike fashion. 'You can tell me later,' she shouted over her shoulder. Amy got up, and after taking a quick shower, dressed in tightly fitting black jeans that hugged her perfect hips smoothly, and a black tee-shirt, embroidered with a large glistening insect.

Brushing out her hair and tying it up in a neat ponytail, she left the bathroom and went to have breakfast.

Joni had made lots of toast, in various shades from light brown to black, and Amy had to hunt through them to find two reasonable pieces. She ate them thickly buttered, and covered with honey, washed down with three cups of strong, black coffee. Joni, who had been on the phone, came into the kitchen as Amy was lighting a cigarette, sitting back replete after the satisfying meal.

'You've taken the best pieces!' she accused laughingly, as she hunted through the toast. 'That was Terry on the phone. He wants us to drive down to Brighton today,' she explained, with shining eyes. Terry Seymour was a tall, handsome young man whom Joni had met a couple of months before, at a party they had thrown in the flat for her birthday. It had been a surprise, arranged by Amy, who had invited everyone she could think of, on condition that they bring a friend. Terry had arrived with somebody from the flat above theirs. He had made a beeline for Joni, monopolising her company all evening.

She had been out with him quite a few times since then. Amy felt secretly sure that Joni and Terry were made for each other.

Gulping down her coffee, Joni rushed to her room to change. Amy decided to spend the day cleaning the flat, and shopping. She cleared the breakfast dishes into the sink, throwing the uneaten toast out of the window into the small garden at the back of the flat, glad that birds were not as fussy as Joni and herself.

As she washed up, thoughts of Matt Cavanagh filled her mind. The sweet summer smell of the flowers he had sent to the gallery filled the flat, it seemed to Amy, with his presence. She knew that she was falling in love with him, but she also knew that he saw her as little more than a child. She pondered for long minutes, correcting this image, but came up with no suitable solutions. Silently chiding herself for wasting time, she sat down and made out a list of the shopping that they needed. Joni rushed into the kitchen, just as the doorbell rang.

'I don't know when I'll be back. We might stay over. Terry's parents live in Brighton—'bye!'

''Bye, Joni! Have a good time,' Amy shouted to Joni's retreating back. The door slammed and the flat was quiet. Amy stood up, and walked through the empty rooms. She felt different today. Frowning, as she tried to define her feelings, she tidied up the bathroom. It looked as though it had been hit by a bomb. Joni was always in a rush.

How nice to be Joni, cheerful, uncomplicated and always making the best of everything. Amy sighed. How dreary she was becoming!

It was Matt Cavanagh's fault. Even now, she still ached for him, and she could not put him out of her thoughts for five minutes. Wandering back into the kitchen, she lit a cigarette moodily and sat down. Perhaps buying a new dress would cheer her up. Yes. She had seen a beautiful green dress when they had been looking for Joni's red shoes. Made of pure silk, it was the colour of the ocean, made up of a number of subtle shades that changed when the wearer moved. Deciding to buy it, Amy shrugged on a black velvet jacket, and grabbing the shopping list and a basket, left the flat.

She stopped for food first, buying exotic and unusual ingredients to liven up her cookery, and then she made her way to the boutique where she had seen the dress. It was still in the window, so she went in. She knew even before she tried it on that it would fit like a dream, and it did. It was disgustingly expensive, but so right for her that she bought it.

She had just left the shop, when she heard somebody calling her name, and turning, she saw Mike Gelder waving from his car window. She walked over to him, smiling.

'Hello. Can I give you a lift?' he offered, as he gazed at her appreciatively.

'Yes, please, Mike, before I spend any more money that I can't afford.' He grinned at her indulgently as she slid into the car.

'Why, what have you been buying?'

'Oh, just a wildly expensive dress—we won't be able to eat for a week!'

Laughing, Mike started the car, and drew away from the curb. They chatted lightly on the way back to Amy's flat. She had known Mike Gelder for just over a year, and they had gone out casually together a few times. He was tall and athletic, and rather handsome, and she knew that he was in love with her. In fact he had proposed marriage already. Amy was fond of him but certainly did not love him, and she could not commit herself to a lifetime as his wife and lover. Because of her youth, he did not press her, but he could not wait for ever. He had loved her from the first moment he had seen her. She was pure and beautiful, and he felt sure that he could make her happy. Feeling impatient that he never seemed to make any headway with her, he said impulsively, 'Come out with me tonight, Amy. We could go for a meal and on to the theatre— there's a new play just opened in the West End, to rave reviews. What do you say?'

'I'm sorry, Mike. I have something else planned.' Amy felt bad about lying to him, but she realised that it would be unfair to go out with him, when her thoughts were filled by Matt Cavanagh. Seeing his face drop, she finally agreed to see him later that week.

Letting herself into the flat, a few minutes later, she was regretting the arrangement. It was unfair, and she should not be so cowardly. When he picked her up she would tell him gently that she loved somebody else, and could not see him any more. It was certainly true, however impossible it seemed after only one meeting, and she prayed for Sunday to come quickly, so that she could see Matt again.

She spent the rest of the day cleaning the flat. Donning an apron and rubber gloves, she cleaned and polished every room until the whole flat shone brightly. By the time the work was finished, she felt hungry and exhausted. So after taking a quick, hot shower to ease her aching muscles, she dressed in a brown floral caftan and set about preparing her lonely dinner. Still, she thought, it was fairer to both Mike and herself not to use him. She made a tasty beef curry, and sat crosslegged in front of the television, eating it. The evening passed quickly and peacefully between watching television and writing to her aunt and uncle in Germany. By the time she went to bed it was midnight—only twelve hours before she would see Matt again.

There was no sign of Joni, but Amy left the hall light on, just in case she returned. After punching her pillows into a comfortable position, she drifted easily into sleep. Sleep filled with dreams of the man she loved.

CHAPTER THREE

SUNDAY dawned bright and sunny, and Amy woke feeling refreshed and alert at eight o'clock sharp. Jumping out of bed, filled with excited anticipation, she opened the curtains and flung open the window to gulp in huge breaths of morning air.

The street was quiet, dozing in a sleepy Sunday atmosphere. Amy loved Sunday, the only day of the week when one could do anything or nothing.

She showered leisurely, humming softly to herself, and slipping on her gown, decided to have breakfast before dressing. Tiptoeing into Joni's room, she found it empty, the bed unused. Lucky Joni, she must be getting on well with Terry's parents. Amy certainly hoped so, because Joni deserved to be happy.

Going into the kitchen, she found herself ravenously hungry, so she boiled some eggs, as well as making her usual toast. She turned on the radio while she was eating, but did not listen because she was trying to decide what to wear. The choice really boiled down to trousers or a skirt. Personally, she would have preferred a skirt, but trousers were more practical, especially if she was going to be spending the afternoon posing for Matt Cavanagh. She gazed into the kitchen mirror, at a loss to understand just what it was that Matt had seen in her that he wanted to paint. She saw nothing. She was just an average, fairly attractive girl. Shrugging as she turned away, she wondered if she would ask him.

She wandered into her bedroom, and examined

her clothes. Work, she thought firmly, was the order
of the day, there was no use thinking or pretending
otherwise. She had certainly had no encouragement
from Matt to think anything else. And that, she
admitted to herself, was the problem. She was fairly
sure that he saw her as little more than an attractive
child, to be indulged, even though he had made her
feel all woman in his company. While to her, he was
the man that she loved. It was true that they had
only been out together once, and Amy had never
been a believer in love at first sight, but nonetheless
she loved him. Her love was new, pure and trusting.
He had taught her desire just by pulling her into his
arms and kissing her. He alone could fulfil this new
desire that he had aroused in her, and Amy was
curious about sex. Many of her friends at school had
experimented with young, pimply boys, with totally
unsatisfactory results, it had seemed to her. Matt
Cavanagh was an older, experienced man, and she
knew instinctively that he would be a passionate,
gentle lover.

Before she had met Matt, Amy had often considered marrying Mike Gelder. He was kind, secure,
and he loved her. But since Matt had kissed her on
that dark and lonely moonlit beach, she realised that
to compromise away her life, never knowing the fever
of a shared love between a man and woman, was
wrong, and could only lead to frustrating un-
happiness. Her whole life had been turned upside
down within two days, but she hoped that she was
willing to take the pain, if she could experience the
ecstasy. Brave and untested principles, but her youth
and untouched spirit held them high.

Shaking her head at the serious turn her thoughts
had taken, Amy finally chose tight, faded denim
jeans, and white tee-shirt. Dressed in them, she

looked tall and voluptuous. She brushed out her hair, leaving it loose. 'Always wear it this way for me,' Matt's harshly spoken words echoed in her head, as she smoothed it back. In the bathroom she applied mascara to thicken her dark lashes, and colourless lip gloss. She needed no other make-up, her complexion being smooth and healthy. Examining herself critically in the mirror, she was satisfied with the reflection it threw back at her. Shining topaz eyes, and lustrous black hair, that fell softly, outlining her long, curved body. If she wanted Matt Cavanagh to see her as a woman, this ought to do the trick.

It was only ten-thirty, and Amy paced around the flat impatiently, before lighting a cigarette and flicking through the Sunday papers. She felt nervous and jumpy and so impatient that she had to force herself to concentrate on the newspaper articles before her eyes. By ten to twelve she was standing by the window, peeping through the curtains, waiting for his arrival. When the doorbell rang at midday exactly, she nearly jumped out of her skin. She walked slowly to the front door, nervously smoothing suddenly damp palms over her hips, and her heart constricted painfully at the sight of him, as she opened the door. Dressed casually in denim jeans that hugged his lean hips and muscular legs, and a checked shirt in red and blue, that emphasised the powerful broadness of his chest, he emitted a raw sexual magnetism that turned Amy's legs to jelly.

'Hello, Amy.' His dark eyes flicked over her unhurriedly, resting disturbingly on the soft curves of her breasts, slim rounded hips and long legs.

Flushing under his inspection, she stammered her reply. 'Hello, Matt. I ... er ... come in ... er ... would you like some coffee?' As he followed her into the flat, she could feel his eyes upon her, and she had

to fight the longing to turn and fling herself into his
arms. He had not touched her, but his steady intense
gaze was an intimate caress, and she felt her body
responding. He filled the room, making it seem
smaller, as he glanced round, taking in the brightly
coloured walls and the chaotic collection of possessions that Amy and Joni had managed to cram into
the room. It was bright and original, and displayed
great artistic flair. Nevertheless, Amy was glad that
she had cleaned and polished so thoroughly the day
before. She made the coffee with shaking hands, and
carried it in to find Matt stretched lazily in an easy
chair, lighting a cigarette. Words stuck in her throat,
and she found herself without a thing to say, at the
sight of him—so dear and familiar, and yet so unknown.

Taking the coffee from her trembling, unresisting
fingers, he smiled, 'Shall I do that?' Deftly he poured
two cups. 'Cream? Sugar?'

'Just cream, please,' she answered, cursing her
own inadequacy.

'Amy, are you afraid of me?' The question was
serious, she realised, looking up and catching the
brooding expression on his face.

'No, I don't think so. I just find you a little overwhelming,' she replied honestly, flashing him a brilliant smile and hoping that she did not sound too
stupid. She probably did. She was aware that she
was no match for him, intellectually, added to which,
the desire she could hardly contain, to throw herself
into his arms, made conversation difficult.

Draining his cup, he uncoiled his long hard body,
and stood up. 'Are you ready?'

'Yes, where are we going?' Amy got to her feet,
tossing back her hair with careless hands, unaware
that the movement drew attention to the firm swell-

ing of her breasts, and that Matt Cavanagh's eyes were drawn darkly to her.

'My studio.' His curt reply was softened by his breathtaking smile as he held out his hand. 'Come on.'

She slipped her hand into his happily, and they strolled out to his car.

His studio was an hour's drive from London, the streets being relatively quiet on Sundays. Matt put her at ease as they drove, enjoying her tinkling laughter at his deliberately amusing conversation, wanting her to be happy in his company.

Soon they were turning off the main road, down the shady, tree-lined drive that led to his house and studio. Amy looked round curiously as the house came into view. It was a large grey stone mansion, with long elegant windows and ivy covering a large part of it. She was enchanted as the car slid to a halt in front of the large oak front door.

'It's lovely!' she breathed. 'How lucky you are to live here.'

'Yes, I appreciate the quiet—London's so noisy and dirty. Come, I'll show you round.'

She slid out of the car, her sandals crunching on the gravel, as they walked to the house.

The entrance hall was huge and high-ceilinged, a large stained-glass window throwing muted, multi-coloured light into the cool green interior. The green carpet in a similar light shade was inches thick, and Amy kicked off her sandals, sinking her toes into the deep luxurious softness of it, and caught Matt's curious glance.

'You don't mind, do you? Shoes are so unnecessary sometimes,' she smiled at him.

He laughed, deep lines etching his brown face.

'Amy, you're beautiful, do whatever you like,' he answered.

The walls were lined with strong, aggressive abstracts, contrasting vividly with the pale paint, and various items of dark wood furniture completed the room. It was quite beautiful, and Amy marvelled, wide-eyed, at his perfect taste.

She followed him through one of the many oak doors that led off the hall, into a cool brown and cream room that was obviously Matt's study.

The walls were covered with books, and in front of the tall windows stood a number of small sculptures, some bronze and some wood, all reflecting the light from their smooth surfaces. A large desk and deeply comfortable leather chair dominated the other side of the room and light, Oriental mats scattered the chocolate-coloured carpet. The room reflected a calm, tasteful atmosphere and she gazed round interestedly.

'Would you like a drink?' Matt's voice cut across her reverie.

'No, thanks, I'd like to get started, I think. Your house is so beautiful, I could spend hours and hours just looking at everything,' she replied candidly.

He smiled at her compliments. 'Thank you. If you're sure about the drink, I would like to get started.' He led the way through a door on the other side of the study, into a startlingly light airy room. His studio had obviously been an outbuilding originally, and the roof had been removed and replaced by a single sheet of glass. The walls were painted white, and the result was stark, clear and bright. Easels, paintings and unfinished sculptures littered the room and a red, velvet chaise-longue was pushed against one wall.

Turning, her eyes bright and enthusiastic, Amy found Matt studying her with an intensity that made

. her shiver involuntarily.

'What shall I do?' she murmured softly, not wanting to break the shimmering spell that seemed to hold both of them, at the moment.

Matt turned away, breathing deeply, breaking the strange contact. 'I'd like you to wear this.' From his outstretched hand hung shimmering golden material. Reaching for it carefully, making sure that her fingers did not touch his, Amy took the dress and shook it out. It was made of a thin, light silky material, unknown to her. The colour of her eyes, it seemed to glow softly in the bright light, like dull gold. Long and straight, it flared out at the bottom, where the gold faded into myriad rainbow colours, that glimmered hypnotisingly.

'It's exquisite,' she breathed, 'it's like a dream! I couldn't possibly wear it. . . .'

'You can and you will,' Matt asserted, becoming suddenly businesslike. 'You can change behind that screen.'

Following the direction of his curt nod, she noticed a large Japanese lacquered screen across one corner of the room.

Feeling suddenly frightened, she turned to him, needing reassurance. 'Matt, I. . . .'

'Amy——' he began impatiently, then noticing her sad, uncertain eyes, he touched her cheek gently, his voice softening. 'Don't look so unhappy. There's nothing to worry about—I won't force you, if you don't want to. I bought that dress many years ago, knowing that when I found the woman who could wear it, I could create something—an idea—that's haunted me for years.' He paused, his eyes scanning her face. 'You are that woman. Do you understand?'

There was a deeper meaning to his words, that she could not grasp, she was sure.

'Yes, I think so,' she whispered. 'I'm sorry, of course I want to wear the dress. I'll go and change.'

Her thoughts raced as she undressed behind the screen. She was merely a part of something else, some dream that had possessed him for many years. For some reason she felt piqued. She was Amy Lawrence and she was not going to let him forget it!

She unzipped the dress and slipped it over her head. It fitted her perfectly, clinging sensuously to her curved female body. She struggled with the zip, finding that she could not reach to fasten it. Damn. She would have to ask Matt to do it for her.

Twirling around, she caught sight of herself in the long mirror that covered one of the screen's panels, and gasped, amazed at her reflection. The dress was a sexual dream. Her smooth golden shoulders rose gracefully from the low neckline, the thin material moulding her lovingly. It reflected the colour of her eyes, making them sleepy and feline, and contrasted vividly with the midnight softness of her hair. The colours swirled down to just below her knees, her long slim legs and bare feet completing the sensual picture. Amy could hardly believe that the dress had turned her into the alluring siren that stared back at her from the glass. She emerged from behind the screen to find Matt at the other end of the studio, mixing some paints.

'Could you zip me up, please?' Her voice sounded small and breathless in the large room.

He turned slowly from his work, and his breath caught in his throat as he saw her. He stood perfectly still, his eyes narrowing as they ran over her. She was achingly lovely, the dress wrapping her body in gold, and desire cut through him fiercely.

He walked over to her slowly, his dark eyes never leaving her face. 'Turn around.' The command was harshly spoken, and she saw the naked desire in his face, as she obeyed. His touch was fire along her spine as he pulled up the zip, and she held herself rigid, willing herself not to sway back against him, wanting to, so much. By the time she turned to face him again his eyes were bland and unfathomable, his control regained. He instructed her politely, his voice cool, to sit on the chaise-longue, and arranged her hair around her shoulders with indifferent grace.

Then, standing behind a large easel, he began to draw. He had told her already that he intended to begin with watercolour sketches, and Amy supposed that this was what he was doing. He worked in silence, his gaze piercing with concentration.

Amy tried to keep perfectly still, and managed to do so for some time, until her neck began to ache with the effort. In the end, she could not stand it any longer.

'Can I move my head, please?'

Matt did not look up. 'Of course. You don't have to sit still.' His reply was absently spoken, and he carried on painting.

'Well, you might have told me!' Amy exploded, angry at his lack of attention, and the wasted effort of sitting perfectly still until she had thought she would scream with the strain.

Matt looked up then, surprised at her outburst. 'Do you want to make some coffee for us?' Amusement threaded his lazy voice, at her outrage.

'You swine!' she choked, and then dissolved into helpless giggles, her anger gone, at the absurdity of the situation.

She made coffee for them both, marvelling at the modern kitchen. Every imaginable labour-saving device was smoothly planned into a vivid red and black, cleverly-designed room. As she waited for the percolator, her thoughts turned to the electric tension that seemed to spring up between them, whenever they were close.

She sensed Matt's self-control, but could not understand the reason for it. The coffee was ready, so she took it back into the studio, and Matt stopped work to drink it. When she asked him about the house, he told her that he had owned it for four years. He had bought it after his first big exhibition. He had renovated it, and designed all the interiors, this task taking him two years.

Amy wondered, without asking, why he had bought such a large house for just one person. This house was obviously a family house, and she pictured in her imagination small dark-eyed children running all over the place. The thought of Matt's children tore at her heart; he would make such a good father, gentle and understanding. And she ought to know, she thought wryly. He treated her like a wayward child, most of the time.

Coffee finished, they continued working, mostly in silence, until Amy's stomach was rumbling with hunger, and she was heartily sick of sitting down. She watched Matt as he worked, committing every inch of his face to memory. His concentration made him totally unaware of her candid surveillance, and she followed his every movement. With his sleeves rolled up as he worked, her gaze was drawn to the strong muscles of his forearms, flexing and rippling under his brown, hair-roughened skin.

Finally, a little after seven, he put down his brushes, stretching wearily, and smiled at her.

'That's all for today. I'll make us dinner.'

'Thank goodness, I'm sick of sitting still. Can I see?' she asked.

'No,' he replied uncompromisingly, 'not until it's finished.'

Amy's snort was frustrated, because she knew that he would not change his mind.

'Shall I change, then?'

'Yes.' He seemed preoccupied. Would she never command his attention?

'Unzip me, Matt.' Her voice was husky and inviting, purposely, but he ignored her, sliding the zip down her back and turning away.

Sighing, she disappeared behind the screen, and changed back into her jeans and tee-shirt. Things could only get better, she thought optimistically, as she hung the gold dress carefully over the screen in the absence of a hanger.

Matt was waiting for her, idly smoking, when she reappeared. 'Forgive me, Amy. When I'm working, I'm totally absorbed.' The quiet persuasion with which he spoke soothed her irritation, and she smiled at him. He could make her happy so easily—a kind word, an intimate glance and she could forgive him anything.

In the kitchen Matt began preparing dinner. Amy wanted to help, but he refused to let her, making her sit down with a glass of wine, while he grilled two succulent steaks and prepared a salad.

'You've done enough work today,' he teased gently, 'sitting like a statue for hours on end.'

They talked about his work over dinner, and having gained his complete attention, Amy was not sure she could handle it. They laughed a lot, and Matt's charm was completely unaffected and natural; he was witty and gentle, finding her honest, serene and incredibly beautiful. After the meal, and rather a lot of wine, he lit a roaring log fire, because the evening had turned quite chilly, and they sat together in front of it, under dim lights, and listened to music. He had a huge collection of jazz records, a taste Amy shared.

It seemed right that she should lay her head against his shoulder, so she did. He put his arm around her, hugging her closer. Smiling up into his face, her eyes filled with dreams, she heard him whisper her name as his mouth came down on hers. His lips were gentle, parting hers with an expertise that made her tremble. The kiss was slow, thorough and unhurried, and she responded fully, kissing him back, and exploring his hard mouth with her tongue. Groaning, he pulled her into his arms, and his kiss deepened, hardening with passion. She heard his heartbeat quicken, racing away as she slid her hands up over his broad chest and around his neck, to twist her fingers into his thick dark hair, pulling him closer.

As his mouth moved caressingly over her throat, Amy knew that this was the moment that she had been waiting for all day. Desire ran through her body like fire — how she wanted him! With shy, trembling fingers she unbuttoned his shirt, needing his skin beneath her fingers, and pulled it from his muscular shoulders, running her hands slowly over his hair-roughened chest. His body gleamed like oiled teak in the dim light, and her mouth went dry as she encountered the molten expression in his half-closed eyes. His breathing was ragged and uneven as he deftly unhooked her bra, and his mouth closed on hers, so sweetly, as his hands slid over her body slowly, almost as if the touch of her soft skin was enough to drive him crazy.

Amy arched her body convulsively as his mouth sought her silk-sheathed breast, a moan of pure pleasure escaping her at his tormenting caress. They both stiffened suddenly, as the telephone began ringing loudly and discordantly. Swearing under his breath, Matt tried to ignore it, but Amy could not.

'You'd better answer it,' she whispered, 'they'll only ring again, and the noise drives me mad!'

Still cursing, Matt got to his feet, snatching up the receiver with impatience. She heard his anger, as he told the person on the other end exactly what he thought of them, and smiled. Glancing at the clock, she saw that it was nearly midnight. She pulled on her clothes quickly, still feeling the ache of desire weakening her limbs and her resistance. Slamming down the phone, Matt came back to her.

'I'd better drive you home,' he said bleakly, pulling on his shirt. 'I'm sorry for what happened, Amy.'

She did not know what to say to him; the evening was suddenly flat. His regret at what had happened between them hurt her. Something of what she was feeling must have shown in her eyes, because with a muttered imprecation he suddenly pulled her into his arms and kissed her hard.

'Sweet Amy,' he murmured. 'Saved by the bell. Come on, let's get you home.'

'Matt . . .' She got no farther, because he placed his finger gently over her mouth and taking her hand, led her out to the car.

She fought back tears of misery and frustration as the car turned on to the open road, and began to pick up speed. She accepted a cigarette from him, and breathed in deeply, thankful for the small measure of relief it gave her. Another disastrous encounter. Matt had wanted her, the fevered urgency of his lovemaking left her with no doubts, but she knew that he was glad now that they had been interrupted before they had both lost control. He regretted what had happened. When they reached her flat, she got out of the car quickly, not wanting to speak to him, sick with the shame of what she saw as his rejection. She ran to the front door, not wanting any contact with him, and shut it quietly behind her. She did not hear the car pulling away, so she walked into the front room, not switching on the light, and peeped through the curtains. She could see Matt sitting in the car. He sat perfectly still, staring straight ahead, and her heart cried out to him. He sat like that for at least five minutes, then shrugging wearily, he switched on the car engine and drove away into the night.

Amy prepared for bed quietly, knowing that Joni was already in, and probably asleep, and slipped into bed. Tears ran silently down her face, sobs racking her body, as she relived the moments of passion in Matt's arms.

The dawn was creeping across the sky like a silent grey cat before she finally drifted into a light, troubled sleep.

CHAPTER FOUR

MONDAY morning was dark and wet. Amy felt dreadful and knew that she looked worse as she entered the gallery, shaking the rain off her umbrella. Joni had not commented on her pale, hollow-eyed look at breakfast, but had chattered on enthusiastically about her weekend in Brighton. Not wanting to talk about her own weekend, Amy had thankfully blessed her cousin's tact.

John Wilson, however, commented bluntly on her appearance.

'Good God, Amy, you look terrible! Are you ill?'

'Well, I don't feel too good . . .' she began.

'Perhaps you should go home and rest,' he cut firmly across her feeble remark.

'No, no, I'd rather stay, if you don't mind, John.' Her voice sounded flat and weary even to her own ears.

John shrugged. 'It's up to you, of course. You're on holiday next week, aren't you? You want to make sure that you get a good rest.' He picked up the phone, and Amy breathed a sigh of relief that the conversation was at an end.

The day dragged by slowly. The unnaturally bright artificial lights in the gallery emphasised the darkness of the wet day outside, making Amy's eyes ache dully. Dressed smartly in a black suit that did nothing to relieve the pallor of her face, she worked mechanically.

By lunchtime she had typed thirty letters, and dealt with as many phone calls. She felt tired and limp from the lack of sleep the night before, and it showed.

She bought some sandwiches from a health-food shop near the gallery, politely declining John's offer of a drink in a nearby pub, and ate them at her desk. Not that she tasted them at all. Her mind was still on Matt Cavanagh. There was something wrong between them, that she could not understand. They were getting to know each other slowly, and they were getting on well, but his withdrawal from and rejection of her was more than she could cope with or accept. His actions were not calculated, she knew, but they were strong and definite, and wounding to her raw, new love.

Shaking her head, she realised that she was being far too introspective, and forcing the situation out of perspective in her own mind, but she could not stop herself. There was nothing between them, except her love. He was thirty years old, and she only eighteen, obviously untouched and unbearably innocent. And because of her immaturity, she could not hope to satisfy all his needs in the sort of deep, lasting relationship she hoped for. The situation was impossible, and she would only make a complete fool of herself, and get her heart broken into the bargain. Perhaps the best thing to do would be not to see him again, to try and forget him. No, that was impossible. She must try to live without him, and although it did not make her feel any better to have made this decision, in a painful way, she was glad. By the time John Wilson returned from lunch Amy was looking and feeling much better, and he noticed.

'You're looking a bit more lively,' he smiled, 'so let's get some work done, shall we?'

Amy laughingly reminded him of all the work she had already done by sticking the large sheaf of letters under his nose for signing. He laughed. She had made her point.

The afternoon passed fairly quickly, attending to routine jobs, but her depression lingered, and at five-thirty she was heartily glad to switch off the phone at the switchboard and cover her typewriter. The rain had not stopped, and grey looming clouds hung low over shiny streets as she ran for her bus.

She kicked off her soaking shoes with a heartfelt sigh of relief as soon as she entered the flat. The air was filled with the tantalising aroma of cooking food, and she sniffed appreciatively, trying to guess what it was. Joni popped her head out of the kitchen on hearing the front door slam, a wooden spoon in her hand.

'Hi, Amy, there's a letter for you on the table, and guess who just phoned for you?'

Amy's heart missed a beat, but she kept her voice steady and carefully disinterested. 'Who?'

'Matt Cavanagh.' Joni scanned her cousin's face eagerly for some response to those magic words, disappointed when none appeared. 'He sounded quite annoyed when I said you weren't here.'

'I don't want to speak to him. If he rings again, would you tell him that I'm not In?' Amy's eyes were unconsciously pleading, her voice low and strained.

'Amy, are you all right?'

Horrified, she felt herself close to tears at Joni's concern.

'Yes, I'm fine, just a little tired, that's all,' she lied. 'What's for dinner? It smells lovely.'

Ignoring the question, Joni scanned Amy's face closely. 'Do you want to talk about it?' she asked sympathetically.

'No, not yet,' Amy murmured weakly, still battling with her threatened tears.

'Well, it's moussaka for dinner, and rather delicious too, if I may say so!' announced Joni, tactfully changing the subject. 'And it will be ready in five minutes.'

As she sat down at the table, Amy noticed a bottle of wine and two glasses. 'Are we celebrating something?' she called to Joni, who was dishing up the meal in the kitchen.

'We are indeed! I've also baked a cake for dessert.' She came in carrying two plates of steaming, aromatic food. 'Terry asked me to marry him this afternoon, and I said Yes.'

'Oh, Joni! I'm so happy for you.' Amy jumped up and hugged her cousin joyfully.

'Hey, mind the food!' Joni giggled, her eyes shining like diamonds in her happy face.

The moussaka was delicious, and they chatted happily about the wedding, drinking each other's health merrily. In the middle of one such toast, the phone rang.

Amy's face paled, and she felt sick.

'I'll answer it,' said Joni firmly, noting her stricken expression. 'And if it's him I'll tell him you're out.'

Amy could not listen to the conversation that ensued when Joni picked up the phone. Maybe it wasn't Matt after all. But Joni's face told her differently, when she re-entered the room.

'It was Matt Cavanagh, and he sounded really suspicious when I told him you were out. He practically called me a liar—his voice is so sexy, though, I could forgive him anything!' Her voice was wistful, and Amy shook her head in exasperation.

The meal was spoiled for her, even the wine had lost its taste. She knew that she was being cowardly, not speaking to Matt, but she could not face him. Acting as though nothing had happened was a strain, but she managed it, and they finished the meal laughing happily, and if Joni noticed any change in Amy, she wisely did not mention it.

Amy insisted on washing up, while Joni got ready to go out with Terry. Feeling so tired and depressed during the day, Amy had cancelled her evening engagement at lunchtime, and now she was heartily relieved that she had done so.

When Joni had gone, not at all happy at leaving her on her own, Amy took a warm shower, feeling some of the tension of the day leaving her tired body, under the hot jet of water.

She slipped on her dressing gown and sat by the fire, feeling incredibly weary, letting herself relax, and feeling her eyes slowly closing. She was just drifting off to sleep when the doorbell rang loudly, making her jump. Sighing, she forced herself out of her comfortable chair, and wandered to the front door yawning groggily. Opening it, she found Matt Cavanagh on the doorstep. 'Let me in Amy, I want to talk to you.' He looked tired, his lean face haggard and strained.

'Go away,' she whispered confusedly, still trying to drag herself out of her sleepy mood. His mouth tightened, and ignoring her, he pushed his way in through the door and walked into the flat. She slammed the front door and followed him, anger stirring inside her at his behaviour.

'What do you want?' she asked belligerently, absently noting how attractive he looked in close-fitting black trousers and a casual black jacket.

'I want to talk to you. Why wouldn't you speak to me on the phone?' He was staring intently at her, and she turned away, not wanting to answer.

How could she tell him that she did not want to speak to him because she loved him and she was frightened of rejection?

'Well?' His voice was uncompromising. 'Is it something to do with last night?' He grasped her shoulders and turned her to face him, his eyes narrowing as they scanned her tired, drawn face, noting the dark shadows beneath her beautiful eyes, with concern. He eased his grip on her.

'No, it's nothing to do with last night,' she lied. 'I just didn't want to speak to you. I'm very tired,' she finished wearily.

'Go to bed. I'll make you some hot milk.' His voice was soothing, and to Amy, irritating.

'Stop treating me like a child—I'm not a child!' she snapped, not moving.

'I know,' he murmured, his eyes darkening as they slid the length of her body intimately, scorching through the thin gown to her nakedness beneath, it seemed to her.

She turned and fled to the bedroom, hearing his low laughter as he went to the kitchen. Lying in bed, with the sheets pulled up to her chin, she assessed her feelings at seeing him again. She was glad. The fact that he cared enough to come and find out why she would not speak to him made her feel warm inside. She had been stupid to imagine that he could be cut out of her life. She wanted to see him, whatever the price.

He walked into the bedroom carrying a cup of steaming liquid, and smiled. 'Drink this!'

She drank every bit obediently, eyeing him over the rim of the cup. It was delicious.

'Lie back and go to sleep. We'll talk some other time.' He leaned over and brushed her mouth gently with his. The temptation to wind her arms around his neck was almost too great to resist, but she was so tired that she could feel her eyes closing even as he kissed her. Matt stood watching her sleep for a long time, his eyes dark and unfathomable in his strong face. Then he quietly left the room, switching off the light, and walked slowly out to his car.

The rest of the week passed quickly. Amy saw nothing of Matt, even though John Wilson had several meetings with him, regarding the exhibition.

On Thursday evening she went for a drink with Mike Gelder, and explained to him gently that she would not be seeing him again. He was hurt and angry, but he accepted it without demur. Amy made sure that he could not do anything else.

Back at the flat, she felt mean and a little cruel, but she had done the right thing, she was sure. Mike's halfhearted anger and quick acceptance of the situation made her wonder just how deep his feelings were, and she felt amazed and disgusted when she remembered how she had considered marrying him. Thoughts of Matt kept her happy, even though she did not know when she would see him again.

On Saturday morning, she was awakened by the telephone, and groaning, she rolled out of bed. It was so persistent, and always seemed to ring at the wrong time. It was Matt.

'You woke me up!' she complained, unable to keep the laughter out of her voice.

'Sit for me today.' His voice was persuasive, low and as sexy as Joni had said. She could feel the goose-pimples down her back when he spoke.

'Yes,' she answered, not needing to think about it.

'I'll pick you up in two hours.'

His conversation was brief and direct, thought Amy, replacing the receiver. He certainly did not waste words.

She took coffee in to Joni, who had also been

wakened by the phone and was complaining loudly about having it taken out before their lives were ruined, then began to get ready.

She chose a brown patterned dress that hugged her figure smoothly and matched her eyes. Studying herself critically in the mirror after applying a light make-up, she was well pleased with the smart, cool reflection that stared back at her.

The germ of a plan was forming in her mind, as she ate some toast—a plan that if it succeeded would certainly stop Matt Cavanagh seeing her as little more than a child. She smiled secretly to herself, hoping that she had the courage to go through with it, and decided to take Joni breakfast in bed.

Humming softly to herself, she boiled some eggs and made more toast, and putting them on a tray with orange juice and coffee, took them into Joni's bedroom.

'Thanks, Amy. I see you got my message.' Amy stared at her blankly. 'Telepathy.' She bit into a piece of toast. 'Mm, lovely—who was that on the phone?'

'Matt Cavanagh.'

'At this time in the morning?' Joni was obviously surprised.

'Yes. He wants me to sit for him again today.'

'And are you going to?'

'Yes. I love him, Joni. I've tried not to, but I just can't help myself,' Amy confided in her cousin, sadly.

Joni sighed. 'I hope everything works out for you, Amy, I really do. Anyway, how could he fail to love you?' she smiled, her voice bright and optimistic suddenly. 'Maybe we can have a double wedding!'

Amy giggled, and left the room, feeling happy at Joni's absurdity.

Matt arrived exactly on time, as usual, looking tall and disturbing in denim jeans and a denim shirt. Amy introduced him to Joni, and they shook hands, Matt smiling down at her, with a lazily sensual look in his eyes that made Joni blush. As they were leaving, Joni whispered to Amy, 'Good heavens, I hope you can handle him!'

Amy laughed. ''Bye, Joni, I'll do my best.'

As they drove Matt flicked her an enigmatic glance, his eyes narrowed against the sunshine that flooded the car.

'You're feeling better?' It was more of a statement than a question, and Amy shook her head, without answering. She did not want to talk about Sunday night, or Monday, and hoped that he would not mention it. It was too embarrassing.

'Cigarette?' It seemed as though he had read her mind, and was not pursuing the subject.

'Yes, please.'

He lit two, passing her one, as he drove. Placing it between her lips was like kissing him. She smiled at her ridiculous thoughts, as she inhaled deeply. The silence stretched between them ominously.

'I'm on holiday next week.' She said this just for something to say, and immediately wished that she hadn't, in case Matt thought that she was angling for an invitation of some sort.

Amusement threaded his voice as he replied. 'Are you going away?'

'I don't know. I may go down to Cornwall to see my grandfather. He's all alone since my grandmother died.' Sorrow filled her voice for a moment.

Changing the subject, Matt suddenly said, 'Amy, did you want to sit for me today?' He was careful and intent, as he waited for her answer.

'Yes.' Her reply was simple and honest, but needing to try and set things straight, she continued, 'I'm sorry about Monday. I thought that it would be better if I didn't see you again . . .' She trailed off lamely. God, she was making a mess of this. Matt did not answer, his eyes remained on the road, his expression blank. 'But when I saw you, I knew that it wouldn't work—that I wanted to see you . . .' she sighed hopelessly.

'Amy, you don't have to explain anything to me.' His reply was quiet and slowly spoken, and she took it to mean that the subject was closed.

She was amazed anew at the peaceful beauty of his house, as it came into sight. 'Does your house have a name?' she asked enthusiastically.

'No, I haven't given it one. The idea always seems somewhat absurd.'

She glanced at him and saw the amusement in his face. 'You're laughing at me,' she smiled as they got out of the car.

'Not really,' he answered gently, taking her arm and guiding her into the house.

Over coffee Matt outlined the work that he hoped to do during the afternoon. Amy listened carefully, watching the movement of his face as he talked. He had told her over dinner, the week before, about his life. He had been born and bred for a position of power. His father had been a hard, wealthy industrialist, who had taught his small son how to take what he wanted, regardless of the consequences.

Matt had left home at sixteen, sickened by his father's way of life, and had travelled the world, the hard way, educating himself en route. Returning to England twelve years later, he was just as hard as his father, but with a compassion and a gentleness that refused to let him take over his father's business.

Cut out of his father's life, he continued doing

what had earned him the money to live when he had been abroad—painting. And now he was becoming well-known and respected in England and America, and he was rich in his own right, honestly, and without crushing the spirit from anybody else. The idea of stealing self-respect for personal gain had disgusted him, and he had had the strength not to take the easy way out and go into his father's business, but to revolt against it and change his way of life, to live by his own principles. He had made it, and Amy admired and respected him.

His face was hard and showed his inner strength clearly, she thought. He was a tough man, with many different facets to his complicated character, facets that she had only glimpsed in her brief time with him.

'Shall we start?' His question cut across her thoughts, and she looked up blankly. 'Where are you, Amy?' A smile softened his eyes as he spoke.

'In your past, but I'm ready to start work,' she answered, jumping to her feet.

In the studio she changed into the golden dress quickly, and Matt zipped it up, pressing his lips to her neck as he did so.

'You're breathtaking,' he murmured huskily, winding her hair round his fingers, and in the magic of the moment she believed him. She sat down, and he took up position behind the easel.

'Matt, will I be able to see it today?' she asked.

'No.'

'When?'

'When it's finished—I've told you.'

She sat silently, knowing that his attention had left her and that he was completely engrossed in his work. She glanced idly around the studio. There were canvases stacked against the walls and the smell of paint was strong but not unattractive.

A couple of hours later they stopped for coffee and thick roast beef sandwiches, which Amy munched hungrily. She felt Matt's eyes on her as they chatted, quiet and watchful, taking in every movement of her graceful body and beautiful face. She watched him too, and slowly but surely, a tense awareness built up between them. It was like a game, thought Amy, hypnotised, her glance hungry, as it rested on his broad shoulders—a game that was moving slowly but inexorably towards its inevitable climax. The climax that she wanted, needed after all this waiting. Waiting that had stretched her nerves, and filled her mind to the exclusion of all else, in the past week.

Draining his cup, Matt lit two cigarettes and passed her one, wordlessly. She wondered why he did not speak. Electricity crackled between them, as she took the cigarette from his fingers, and she flinched from the contact.

Passing her tongue over dry lips, she knew that she had to break the silence before she screamed.

'Where did you buy this dress?' It was the first thing that came into her head, and her voice shook as she spoke.

He answered without taking his eyes from her face. 'Morocco. It's a gift of love.'

She digested this slowly, but it was far too cryptic for her to make any sense of. Stubbing out her cigarette with trembling fingers, she stood up abruptly.

'Shall we get on?' Her voice was false and bright, and her inability to handle the situation between them was obvious.

Matt's mouth twisted. 'You're frightened of me.'

She shook her head silently in denial.

UNTAMED WITCH 59

'No need, my love. I believe we've been through this before.' His voice was curt, his words clipped and precise, and Amy felt hurt as he turned away and strolled lazily towards the studio.

She followed him, feeling like a ticked-off child, near to tears. She sniffed loudly, wanting his comfort, but he ignored her. Defiance lifted her head as she sat down before the easel.

They worked for long hours, until the light was fading. Matt was silent, his mouth hard, and Amy was angry. She wanted him so much that she ached. The only fear he inspired in her was that of rejection. His constant implication that he thought her a child was wearing her patience thin. Inexperienced, perhaps, but a child she was not, and she would show him. She had asked nothing of him, he had made all the running since they had met. That was going to change.

She glanced up to find him smiling at her. 'Are you planning a murder?' he asked amusedly, his anger gone.

Amy carefully smoothed out her expression. She had been unaware of frowning darkly, her eyes angry, but Matt had noticed, and was intrigued. 'Mind your own business!' she snapped, still annoyed with him, and he rocked with silent laughter.

'We've finished for today, the light's going. You'd better change.' He looked bigger in the dim light, and Amy's heart began to thud painfully at the enormity of what she intended to do. He stretched wearily, and she heard him lighting a cigarette as she slipped behind the screen. She had forgotten to ask him to unzip the dress, and she had to struggle with it. She managed to pull it down far enough to be able to squeeze out of it with difficulty, then she stripped off the rest of her clothes.

She studied her nakedness in the mirror. Her breasts were firm and round. Dear God, she prayed silently, please let him want me. She loved Matt so much that if he rejected her this time the humiliation would be too much for her to bear. She stepped out from behind the screen.

He was at the other end of the studio, his back turned, whistling softly as he cleaned some brushes. Amy cleared her throat nervously, her heart pounding so loud that she was sure he must hear it.

'Matt . . .'

He turned towards her slowly, freezing stock-still as he saw her.

Her eyes were huge and unconsciously pleading.

'I want you . . . love me.'

His dark glance was hungry as it slid down over her naked body. Her skin gleamed pearl in the rapidly fading light, her black hair a vivid outline to her soft curves.

He let out a long, shuddering breath.

'Dear God, Amy . . .' he groaned softly.

'I want you, Matt——' Her voice was low and inviting, and he covered the distance between them with long strides and pulled her into his arms. His mouth found hers with devastating precision, and she pressed against him, weak with thankfulness and love.

'Amy, you know this is madness,' he muttered hoarsely against her hair. But even as he spoke, his strong, lean hands were sliding hungrily over her body, caressing her with gentle abrasion.

Swinging her into his arms, he carried her out of the studio and up the stairs to his bed. He held her effortlessly, and she wound her slim arms around his neck, pressing soft kisses against his face as they moved.

He laid her on the bed gently, and with his eyes

never leaving her flushed face, began undressing.
Muscles rippled under smooth, tanned skin as he
moved, then he was beside her, reaching for her, the
need undisguised in his face and his hands. With his
mouth urgent on hers, the weight of his body pressed
her into the soft deepness of the bed. She moaned
softly, shuddering breaths shaking her, as his long
fingers played over her, stroking and tormenting her
expertly, until her whole body was on fire. He arched
over her, his lips at her throat, his breathing painful
and uneven, his powerful body taut with uncon-
cealed desire.

His lovemaking was slow and demanding, but
gentle, and Amy felt no fear, only burning pleasure
as his mouth moved to her breasts. Her blood ran
faster, boiling in her veins, as she arched her body
to meet his lips.

Her hands moved instinctively over him, learning
how to give him pleasure, his skin smooth and hard
beneath her fingers.

He lifted his head from her breasts then, black,
molten fever in his eyes, and her name on his lips
as he bent to possess her mouth once more. Amy's
arms went tightly round him, crushing his broad
hair-roughened chest to her aching body, and she
was lost. The musky male smell of him filled her
nostrils, making her senses reel, and lying beneath
him the fire beat higher in her, and all coherent
thought was lost.

A long time later Matt rolled on to his back,
breathing deeply, his chest still heaving, and pulled
her into his arms. He stroked her hair gently and she
lay still, her head against his chest, listening to the
heavy thunder of his heart. Contentment and a
sensual weakness filled her.

'I love you, Matt,' she whispered, unable to stop

the words forming on her lips.

His arms tightened around her. 'Sweet Amy,' he murmured, his mouth against the soft cloud of her hair. She kissed his shoulder.

'I'm hungry,' she remembered.

He looked down at her, his half-closed eyes, dark and gentle. 'So am I, let's have dinner,' he answered, his mouth curved in a lazy smile.

'Did I hurt you?' he asked.

'Only a little, and it soon passed.' She turned her head away, blushing furiously.

'You're so beautiful, Amy,' he murmured softly, his hand slipping possessively over her naked breast. 'You smell like summer, warm and scented.' He kissed her mouth tenderly, his arms closing around her, strong and protective.

They lay like that for some time, both needing the warmth and closeness. The room was dark, the breeze from the open window cool and refreshing.

In the end hunger drove them both to get up.

'My clothes are in the studio,' giggled Amy.

'Wear this.' Matt tossed her his shirt. She pressed it to her face, and she could smell the clean, male scent of him. It was big, but fastened; it was quite respectable, if a little short. He passed her a cigarette, and she stood gazing out of the window as she smoked. She was glad that they were lovers. There would be no coldness between them again. She loved him with all her heart, everything that had happened between them seemed right and beautiful. She never wanted to leave him.

He came and stood behind her, his arms sliding around her waist. 'Matt, what time is it?' she asked.

'After ten. Stay with me, Amy.'

She felt weak at the desire and the need in his voice.

'I want to,' she answered simply, smiling as his arms tightened around her. They went downstairs, hand in hand.

Amy cooked dinner, and Matt lit the fire, set the table and opened the wine. Contentment stretched between them like a tangible cord.

They were both ravenous by the time Amy dished up perfectly cooked chicken in a rich sauce, with potatoes and vegetables, followed by cheese and strong black coffee.

Later they sat in front of the fire replete, talking in low voices, smiling at each other, supremely happy. Finally, with a groan of impatience, Matt reached for her. Desire flared up between them sweetly, and pulling her to her feet, he lifted her into his arms and carried her upstairs.

Amy awoke next morning feeling strange and disorientated. She looked round the unfamiliar room, confused for a moment, then the events of the night before came flooding back. She stretched like a cat, a languorous warmth filling her body, her lips curving in a soft smile. Their lovemaking had been fiery and urgent, but filled with the same innate gentleness that ran through all Matt's actions. She had drifted into sleep, warm and secure in his arms, revelling in the sweet bodily contact.

She turned over and reached for Matt. He was not there, his side of the bed cold and empty. She was wondering where he was when he walked into the bedroom, carrying a tray. Wearing only tight jeans, he looked strong and disturbingly male, and Amy's pulses raced at the sight of him.

'You're awake at last,' he smiled down at her. 'It's after twelve.'

'I don't believe you! How long have you been up?' Her voice was incredulous as she gazed up at him.

'About half an hour. I've brought you some coffee and some toast.' He leaned over her, his lips brushing hers slowly. 'I couldn't bear to wake you. You sleep like a baby, serene and untroubled. Beautiful.'

She bit into a deliciously crisp slice of toast, after sitting up and covering herself modestly with Matt's shirt, and sipped the strong refreshing coffee.

Everything tasted different, brighter, with more flavour. Matt watched her, the smouldering look in his eyes leaving her in no doubt about his feelings. When she had finished her breakfast and was leaning back contentedly licking her lips, he took both her hands in his.

She was so achingly lovely, she touched his soul and he needed her commitment. In two months he would be free—free to ask—he could not wait.

'Amy, I want to marry you. It . . .'

He got no farther, because Amy flung her arms around his neck, love burning in her golden eyes.

'I love you, Matt, and I want to marry you more than anything in the world.' Her voice was light and breathless.

His arms closed around her, hugging her close, and then his mouth found hers and silence reigned for a long time in the bright sunlight-flooded room.

Finally Matt put her away from him with faintly unsteady hands and lit a cigarette. He breathed in deeply, regaining control, and smiled at her. Amy's heart turned over at his smile. It was warm, tender and loving.

'As I was about to say, we'll . . .' He broke off, cursing darkly as the telephone shattered their conversation, shrill and insistent, and Amy giggled helplessly, snuggling against him as he talked.

Everything was so right, so perfect. She had expected no commitment from him, although if she

was honest, she had hoped secretly that he would
fall in love with her, and ask her to marry him. The
future stretched out before her, a lifetime with Matt
as his companion and lover, and maybe, some time
in the future, as the mother of his children. The
thought of bearing Matt's children sent shivers of
ecstasy down her spine. She would make him happy,
so happy that he would never regret for a single
second asking her to share his life with him.

She spread her fingers over his chest, delighting in
the short crisp hairs that tickled her palms. But
gazing up into his face she saw that he was worried,
his eyes concerned and faintly irritated, and her
hands dropped as he promised to be over in a couple
of hours, and slammed down the receiver.

'Matt . . .?'

He looked at her blankly for a second.

'I'm sorry, Amy, I have to go out. That was Joe,
an old friend. His wife has walked out on him and
he's desperate. I have to go to him, he needs help
and I can't let him down.'

'Of course.'

Noting the sadness in his voice, Amy turned her
head away, unwilling to let him see the disappointment and the selfish desire for him to stay, in her
eyes. As if sensing her withdrawal, Matt tilted her
chin with gentle fingers and stared into her face.

'Oh, Amy, Amy, I hate to leave you now. I'm
sorry, we have so much to talk about, I know, but
I'm afraid for Joe's safety if somebody doesn't go to
him . . .'

Amy stopped him with her mouth, disgusted at
her own selfishness.

'You must go. Forgive me, Matt, I'm so greedy
for your company that I can't think straight.'

Matt was still staring into her eyes, wanting to

give her a promise, something to make her feel less lonely.

'Let's go away for a week,' he said suddenly. 'You're on holiday, aren't you? We could fly to Crete tomorrow, what do you think?'

The idea took her breath away and she was silent for a moment. The thought of a whole week in his company, on a sunny romantic island, was devastating.

'Yes—yes, I'd love to. Are you always so fast-moving?' she laughed, still breathless.

'If you always plan your life in advance it becomes rather boring. Acting on impulse, I guess it comes naturally to me,' he shrugged.

'I must be awfully boring, then,' she answered with a smile.

'No, Amy,' his voice was serious, 'never boring. Your life is only just beginning. You're like a bird on the edge of the nest, about to fly away. Take your life and make it your own—if you don't, someone will take it for you.' He laughed then at the maudlin turn of his thoughts, and Amy knew that he was thinking about his father. He kissed her hard. 'You'll come with me to Crete, then?'

'Yes.'

'Right, let's get moving!'

Amy felt dazed, but wildly happy as he left her to shower and dress. He made it sound so easy to make a decision on the spur of the moment and carry it out. Maybe it was. Loving him and knowing him, was showing her a completely different life-style from her own. His life seemed magical, and she wanted to share it.

Matt re-entered the bedroom half an hour later to find her brushing out her hair. He took the brush from her unresisting fingers and pulled it gently through the wild blackness.

'It's all fixed. We leave Heathrow at five tomorrow, arriving just after nine. Your hair is fantastic,' he added inconsequentially. 'Raven's wings fluttering down your back.'

She turned to him. 'Matt—it will be all right?' She was worried.

'Sweet Amy, we'll have the time of our lives. You'll be happy, I promise.'

'Where will we stay?' Reassured, she was beginning to feel excited.

'It's up to you, my love. An hotel or a small villa that belongs to a friend. Which will it be?'

'The villa,' she answered promptly. 'Then I'll have you all to myself.'

He swung her into his arms joyfully, kissing her face with gentle lips.

'I'll drive you home and I'll call round tonight,' he murmured against her mouth, punctuating his words with hungry kisses.

'Yes,' she managed weakly before his kiss deepened, and words were not needed.

When she got back to the flat there was no sign of Joni. Blissfully happy, she wandered about, not wanting to do anything but think about Matt, and the beauty of the love between them.

Finally she ran a hot bath, a luxury which she usually had to forgo in favour of a quick shower, and lay soaking in the soft, scented water for nearly an hour before rousing herself to get out and prepare dinner.

She had just finished washing up when the doorbell rang, and she ran to the door joyfully, knowing it to be Matt, flinging it open and nearly knocking him off balance as she went into his arms.

'Hello, my love,' he said softly, touched and amused by her extravagant greeting.

'Matt, I've missed you so,' she laughed, pulling him inside. 'I thought you'd never come!'

She had not noticed the flowers, perfect red roses, until he handed them to her, a slight smile curving his strong mouth. Ridiculously, she felt tears welling up into her eyes at this beautiful gesture.

'Kiss me,' she begged, not wanting to cry, needing him to so much. Taking her face between his cupped hands, his eyes burning with dark desire as they rested on her upturned face, he lowered his head slowly and found her mouth.

She felt him tremble at her passionate response and his hands left her face to slide over her shoulders and around her, to crush her closer to his body. Aroused by this obvious need, Amy pressed herself against him, her hands tangling in the darkness of his hair, unwilling and unable to let him go.

Finally he put her away from him, gently but firmly, and walked slowly to the other side of the room.

'Matt?'

She stared at him as he turned to face her. He was breathing deeply, his control regained, but lines of strain and weariness were apparent in his face.

'How about some coffee?' he asked lightly, reaching for his cigarettes, his eyes veiled.

Amy frowned at him, feeling uneasy.

'Of course, I'll make some now.'

Turning, she walked slowly into the kitchen, a strange worry gnawing away inside her. Had she done something wrong? While waiting for the coffee, she put her flowers in a vase, sniffing them appreciatively. Such lovely flowers, and Matt had brought them for her—nothing could be wrong.

Pushing her vague worries aside, she took the tray of coffee into the lounge.

'Would you like something to eat?' She studied him with smiling eyes as she asked. Still wearing tight denim jeans teamed with a dark shirt and jacket, he looked strong and lean, but his face was tired and distant.

'No,' he shook his head slowly. 'Sit down, Amy, I have to talk to you.'

She poured coffee for them both, and after handing a cup to Matt, she curled up at his feet and gazed up at him expectantly.

'I won't be able to take you to Crete,' he said flatly.

'Why?' Her question was automatic; his harshly-spoken statement had hit her like a bomb, and she was reeling from the blow.

'I have too much work to do. I'll be very busy before the exhibition,' he answered distantly, his mouth hard and uncompromising. Amy gazed at him, her confusion turning to anger at the casual way he hurt her.

'Too busy to take me away for a week?' she demanded, her golden eyes flashing.

Matt did not answer. His face was proud and closed, an arrogant mask. Amy scrambled to her feet, her temper lost. She would not let him shut her out, not after last night. She shook his shoulder desperately.

'Tell me,' she insisted. 'Tell me why you're too busy to take me away. Did you ever have any intention of going to Crete, or did you say it just to get rid of me this morning?'

She stared at him hysterically, waiting for his answer, praying with her heart that he would not destroy her by admitting that he had wanted her gone, and had been prepared to use false promises to make her leave.

'You begin to sound like a nagging wife,' Matt finally replied, cruelly and so casually, his face still cold, his eyes unfathomable.

Amy flinched, tears welling up in her eyes and blinding her.

'You swine!' she choked.

Unable to stand being near him a moment longer, she turned and fled from the room. She pulled open the front door of the flat, and ran through the main door into the street. Uncaring for her own safety, and still crying uncontrollably, she stumbled across the road, not even hearing the blaring horns of cars swerving to avoid her. She could not believe that Matt was so cruel and hurtful. Confused, she stepped on to the main road, jumping back involuntarily as a van nearly knocked her down. The driver was shouting at her and she turned away quickly, colliding with Matt.

'Dammit, Amy, you're going to kill yourself!' he grated furiously, his hard fingers closing round her upper arms as he pulled her roughly on to the pavement.

'Leave me alone,' she muttered dully, trying without success to pull herself from his grasp.

Ignoring her, he guided her back to the flat, and glancing up at him through her tears Amy saw that his face was bleak and angry. He did not loosen his grip on her until they were inside, and then he pushed her into a chair. Still silent, he poured her a cup of coffee and handed it to her, watching her carefully, with narrowed eyes. The anger seemed to leave him as he watched her drink the coffee. He shook his head wearily.

'Amy . . .' he began, his voice gentle and low. She sensed his regret and cut across him.

'Matt, you don't have to say anything. It's my

fault. I lose my temper so easily. But I was so looking forward to going away with you. I know now that it wasn't real—just a dream. I'm sorry,' she finished sadly, her head bent. There was nothing more to say to him.

He stared at her for a long moment and drew a deep breath. 'It's not your fault, Amy, you know that—I lied to you. I'm not too busy to take you away, and God knows I want to take you to Crete, but you must think of yourself, your reputation—we're not yet married. Do you understand?'

She raised her head to look at him. 'I don't give a damn for my reputation,' she said softly, some of the brilliance returning to her eyes, 'if it means I can be with you. I love you, Matt, I need you and I want to be with you. Please take me to Crete—please!'

'Amy,' he groaned softly, 'you put me in an impossible situation, can't you see that?'

She walked over to him slowly, her beautiful eyes pleading with him. She reached up and touched his face. 'Please, Matt,' she whispered. 'I'll make you happy, I promise.'

Standing on her toes, she pulled his head down and began kissing his mouth. He could not resist her and with a groan of exasperation mingled with desire, he pulled her into the strong circle of his arms.

When he finally lifted his head, Amy knew that she had won. His dark eyes glittered beneath their heavy lids as he gazed down at her, and she smiled at him with languorous eyes.

'Please take me to Crete, Matt. I know what it means and I've made my decision. We are going to be married, after all,' she finished persuasively.

Matt shook his head helplessly, the strain gone from him.

'You little witch,' he murmured softly. 'I can't deny you, especially when I want it so much myself.'

'Oh, Matt, thank you!' She flung her arms around him happily. 'You won't regret it. I promise,'

'I know I won't, my love,' he replied gently, his hands moving in her hair. 'But I don't want you to have any doubts either.'

'I don't, I promise,' she said, triumphant with success.

She would never doubt Matt again because he had put her reputation before his own desire, and had been willing to let her hate him rather than reveal this sacrifice.

Matt left soon after and she went straight to bed. There was still no sign of Joni, but it was still early and Amy was not worried. She lay in bed thinking of Matt. His friend had received a telephone call from his wife, and whether or not it worked out for them, at least Joe was not desperate now. Matt was so kind and so honourable, she thought as she fell asleep.

The next morning Amy woke early. The weather was bright for a change, the sun shining high in an azure sky. She breakfasted quietly without disturbing Joni, then showered and dressed in jeans and a green silk blouse. Slipping her feet into flat sandals, she left the flat noiselessly.

At exactly eleven Matt's car drew up in front of her. They had agreed to meet and have lunch on the river. Happy to be together, they strolled along the river bank after their meal, before driving to Matt's house to collect his luggage. Amy watched as he packed a small case and collected a large sophisticated camera and some painting equipment. Then they locked up the house and drove to Kensington. Amy felt at peace, happy at the prospect of Matt's company for a whole week, and giggled as she imagined Joni's reaction to the news. As far as she knew, Amy was barely on speaking terms with Matt.

When they reached the flat a little over an hour later, Joni greeted them cheerfully from the kitchen.

'Hello, you two. I've just made some coffee, will you have some?'

'Yes, please, Joni. I'll give you a hand.'

Amy followed her into the kitchen, shutting the door behind them.

'What's all this?' Joni's eyes were curious as they rested on Amy's happy face.

'Oh, Joni, everything is so beautiful! Matt asked me to marry him, and we're flying to Crete this afternoon, for a week's holiday. I can hardly believe it!' she finished, her eyes shining.

'Phew! Never a dull moment for you! I'm so glad, Amy—you deserve it!'

Joni hugged her happily, laughing. 'Maybe we will have the double wedding after all. Crete—you lucky devil! I'm green with envy.'

Still laughing together, they carried the coffee into the lounge, and Amy drank hers quickly, leaving Matt and Joni chatting, as she went to pack.

Singing to herself, she gathered together a number of thin summer dresses, lingerie, jeans, her bikini and a couple of evening dresses. She packed them deftly, adding accessories and toiletries, and locked her case.

She stuffed her handbag with her passport and some money and then changed. For the journey she decided to wear a cream lightweight linen suit, with a brown silk blouse, and slender-heeled cream sandals. Applying light make-up, and plaiting her hair into a long, thick rope hanging down her back, she knew that she looked cool and poised. Just before joining the others, she slipped three slim gold bangles round her wrist and attached large gold studs to her earlobes. This small touch completed her sophisticated appearance, and she walked confidently into the lounge. Matt's eyes darkened disturbingly as they lingered on the attractive picture she made, walking gracefully into the room.

Joni's reaction was more forthright. 'You look gorgeous, Amy. That suit is perfect for travelling.'

'Talking of which . . .' interposed Matt smoothly, glancing at his watch, 'we'd better be leaving.'

He uncoiled his long body gracefully and stood up, his powerful presence dominating the small room. Amy's mouth went dry, as her glance flicked over the slim-fitting black trousers and casual black velvet jacket, accentuating his powerful body and dark colouring.

Flashing Joni a devastating smile, he carried Amy's case to the car, tactfully leaving the girls to say goodbye. Still reeling under the force of Matt's intensely male personality, Joni looked dazed as she hugged Amy tightly.

'Be happy, love, and enjoy yourself.'

'I will, and I'll send you a postcard,' answered Amy, hugging her back.

'If you've got time,' retorted her cousin impishly, as they walked to the front door.

Sliding into the car, Amy fastened her seat-belt and they drove away. Halfway to the airport, Matt pulled off the road, and she turned towards him, wondering what was wrong. Some fault in the car, perhaps. But he reached for her, sliding his arm along the back of her seat impatiently. She caught the expression in his eyes, a smile widening her mouth as his lips touched hers.

He pulled her into his arms then, both of them uncaring of the discomfort, as the fiery passion between them strained them closer. Amy moaned softly as his lips moved to her throat, throwing back her head in pleasure, before he possessed her lips again, his kiss deep and drugging.

Finally he put her away from him, breathing heavily. 'I needed that,' he muttered, lighting two cigarettes with strangely unsteady hands. 'I'm starving for you, Amy.'

His darkly burning glance confirmed his ardent words, and she quivered in response, unable to answer him. The rest of the drive to the airport was uneventful, and their plane left practically on time.

Landing at Herakleion Airport a little over four hours later, Amy, flushed and excited, gulped in huge breaths of warm, foreign-smelling air. Even at that late time in the evening, the heat was almost tangible. Matt had arranged for a hired car to be ready for them when they arrived, and as they drove from the low airport building Amy guessed that this week spent with Matt would be one of the most important in her life. She would remember it all her days, often reliving the pure and uncomplicated beauty of it, sometimes with pain, but more often with wonder, and deep pleasure.

The drive to the villa was long and dusty. Amy's suit was creased and grubby, and perspiration trickled stickily down the back of her neck. But even this physical discomfort could not detract from the joy that she felt, just to be alive and in love.

Matt had discarded his jacket, and opened his shirt, and not repressing the urge, Amy slid her hands teasingly over the short dark hair that matted his chest, laughing softly at his immediate response. The land around them was dry and green, and the sea glimmered brightly as the car sped down the coast road.

A little after ten they reached the villa. Perched on the side of a cliff facing a breathtaking view of the Mediterranean, it was small, low and dusky pink. Wooden shutters were closed over all the windows, giving it a sleepy look. Shrubs and scarlet bougainvillea rambled tropically around the villa, and it was exquisitely charming.

Jumping out of the car, her tired stickiness forgotten, Amy walked to the edge of the cliff ledge and gazed towards the horizon. The moon, round and yellow, was rising over the sea, splashing the water with a sparkling trail of light. The night air was warm and fragrant, crickets breaking the silence noisily, and glancing down to the bay, she could see the lights of the small village below, faint strains of music drifting up on the breeze.

She felt Matt's presence before his arm slipped round her shoulders.

'It's beautiful,' she whispered, turning towards him.

'Not as beautiful as you are,' he replied, claiming her lips gently. They walked through the garden to the villa. Matt had switched on the lights, and their cases stood just inside the door. The lounge was large, with whitewashed walls, and a cool marble floor. Delicate wicker furniture including a huge cane rocking-chair scattered the room.

The kitchen was small but practical, and as she opened the large refrigerator Amy gasped. It was filled with food, fruit juice and milk. Opening one of the cupboards next to it, she found bread, coffee and canned food. She walked into the lounge, astonished.

'How . . .?'

'I rang Spiros, after I rang the airport. He told me where the key would be, and said that he'd bring some food.' Matt smiled, amused at her surprise. 'I think of everything, my love.'

Taking her arm, he propelled her out of the lounge through another door, showing her the bathroom.

'There are two bedrooms,' he began, his voice suddenly businesslike. 'One for each of us. It's up to you . . .'

'I want to share yours,' Amy cut in shyly, glad that in his respect for her he had offered her a separate bedroom, giving her the choice, not pushing her. He had brought her here to share his company, to make her happy, not to force her into a situation that she might not have wanted, and love for him filled her heart.

'I'm glad,' he answered, his voice low and sincere. 'But you know that it's there if you want to use it.'

The rest of the evening passed quickly. They were both hot and weary from travelling, and after taking cool refreshing showers, they ate a huge meal, after which Matt suggested a stroll.

Arm in arm they walked along the cliffs, staring at the sea, and at each other. The night sky was black velvet scattered with diamonds, the air was intoxicating, and both felt the magic that surrounded them.

By the time they got back to the villa Amy could hardly keep her eyes open; she was utterly exhausted. Folding her against the hard warmth of his chest, Matt kissed her forehead softly and told her to sleep. Holding her in his arms, he watched her serenely beautiful face, calm and vulnerable in rest, for long hours, before sleep finally claimed him.

The week sped by like a shining dream, and they filled their days to the limit. They drove all around the island, Matt taking photographs of the incredible scenery and of Amy. They swam together in the sea, and lay sunbathing for hours on the pale, powdery beach. Driving to Herakleion, they visited the museum and the busy, thronging bazaar, where Matt bought Amy dozens of little presents, just to see her face light up when he gave them to her. They walked through the Minoan ruins at Knossos, silent with awe at the magnificence around them.

Amy was proud and surprised at the fluency of Matt's Greek as he chatted to the local people.

In the evenings they would visit small tavernas, sampling exotic Greek dishes, and watching the impromptu dancing from young men, who would get up from their tables to dance athletically and clap enthusiastically.

Or sometimes they would sit under multi-coloured lights at the outdoor café on the edge of the harbour, chatting to people who would come to their table, somehow attracted to the tall, charming man and his beautiful companion.

Returning to the villa every night, tired but bliss-fully happy, they would make love. It was fiery and sweet and shook them both to the core of their souls. They were one.

Inevitably, the last day came all too quickly, and there seemed to be a desperation in all they did. They spent the day doing everything that they could think of, and the evening saying goodbye to their newly-acquired friends. There was a sadness about it that made Amy cry like a baby on their way back to the villa for the last time. The fever was in their lovemaking too, that last night.

'Love me, Amy,' Matt groaned as she came to him.

'I do, Matt. I always will,' she whispered against

his strong throat, and it did not matter that his hands moved roughly, because she felt the desperation as well, and responded passionately, her fingers stroking the smooth skin of his back.

Their arrival back in London was flat and grey. It was raining, and they both looked absurdly brown in the grim light. They drove to her flat in silence, both sensing that something was at an end between them. Before she got out of the car Matt pulled her into his arms, kissing her fiercely.

'I'll call you,' he promised, and she nodded sadly, unable to speak.

Once inside the flat, she dropped her case and burst into tears. A strange sense of foreboding filled her, as she told Joni later. 'I wanted it to last for ever, nothing could touch us there.'

CHAPTER FIVE

AMY caught the bus to work the next day, still feeling miserable. Another Monday, she thought wearily, as she walked into the gallery. John Wilson was obviously glad to see her.

'Thank God you're back, Amy. The temp I had was totally incompetent, I was screaming at her by Friday.'

Amy sighed, as she looked at the work piled up on her desk.

'Did you go away?' John asked, noticing her tan.

'Yes, I went to Crete,' she answered absently, scanning a letter, as she took off her coat.

'Well, you look marvellously healthy, you needed a break.' He turned away towards his office, his mind back on work. 'Oh, by the way, there's some stuff coming in today for the Cavanagh exhibition. Any chance of some coffee?' This was his parting shot as he went into his office. Amy smiled and plugged in the kettle. Obviously nothing had changed while she had been away. She felt different, and somehow she had expected everything to change with her. The kettle boiled, and she made the coffee, taking John's into his office, then she started work, attacking the huge backlog with determination.

Matt and his work arrived late in the afternoon. Huge wooden crates heralded his arrival. He looked strong, lean and alert in a dark pin-striped suit, and Amy smiled at him, her heart in her eyes, as he walked in.

Her smile brought out the sun, he thought, his

eyes scanning her darkly, taking in the cool, grass-green dress that fell softly over her slender body, and her long slim legs.

'My word, Miss Lawrence,' he said softly, his voice teasing. 'Is Mr Wilson in?'

'Yes, I'll show you through.' She could not control the laughter in her voice as they walked to John's office.

'I can hardly keep my hands off you,' Matt muttered, as she opened the door. Blushing warmly, she returned to her desk.

The week sped by. Amy had more than enough work to keep her busy. Matt's exhibition was set up slowly, and by the end of the week everything was ready for the opening. She saw a great deal of him in the gallery, and he took her out to dinner mid-week.

For the opening party Amy decided to wear the ocean-green dress that she had bought just after their first meeting. She spent hours getting ready, alone in the flat. Joni had left early that morning to spend a week in Brighton with Terry's parents, discussing the wedding, and Amy missed her help and advice.

She applied more make-up than usual, and threaded small silk flowers into her hair. She knew that she looked attractive, the shimmering dress clinging gently, and her eyes shining in her delicately flushed face.

Arriving at the party, she shrugged off her fur wrap and tidied her hair with trembling fingers, excitement at seeing Matt fluttering in her stomach. After checking every aspect of her appearance, she took a deep breath and stepped into the throng. It was obvious that the exhibition was going to be a huge success, and she felt proud and happy.

She was claimed immediately by John, who was

looking very pleased with himself, and who whistled extravagantly at her.

'You look beautiful,' he said, handing her a drink. Amy murmured an appropriate response, and looked round the gallery for Matt, not really listening to John's enthusiastic chatter. He was immediately distinguishable, his proud, dark head and powerfully broad shoulders instantly recognisable, and her heart skipped a beat as she caught sight of him. He looked tall and commanding in a close-fitting dark suit, expertly tailored to his powerful body, his expression was sardonic and slightly bored, and he scanned the room impatiently, as if waiting for something. She began to make her way towards him, a gentle smile curving her mouth. But before she could reach him, a woman who had been on the perimeter of the group he was surrounded by moved in on him suddenly, taking his arm possessively. A sleek, beautiful redhead, she was stroking the strong muscles beneath the dark suit with scarlet fingernails, as she gazed into his face.

Amy felt sick to her stomach, jealousy ripping through her sharply as she watched the woman laughing—a low seductive laugh, at something that Matt had said. She was beautiful, of course, her body long and supple as it curved against Matt's. Her dress was a tight sheath of black velvet, a perfect foil to her red hair—rioting tousled curls that framed her perfect oval face, and softly inviting scarlet lips. Amy turned away, unable to watch, as the woman wound slim white arms covered with expensive jewellery up around Matt's neck. She did not want to see if the woman kissed him. Had she continued watching, she would have seen Matt gently but firmly put the woman away from him immediately, muttering what was obviously a reprimand, because she pouted angrily and turned away from him.

The party was suddenly too bright, too garish. Conversation seemed to be getting louder and louder, and Amy wanted to put her hands over her ears to block it out. She stumbled towards the door, feeling physically sick, needing to leave. But suddenly Matt was beside her, his hand on her shoulder, her name on his lips, and dark concern in his eyes.

'Amy, where are you going?'

'Home,' she answered shortly, wondering how he dared to touch her after being in somebody else's arms.

'Why, what's the matter?' he demanded. 'I've been waiting for you to get here. I was worried about you . . .'

'Matt, get me a drink, darling.' The redhead had followed him across the room, her eyes soft and misty as she made her plaintive request. Her scarlet talons closed around his arm again, like a sleek bird of prey pouncing on its victim. Except that Matt was nobody's victim, as he proved by removing the woman's arm from his at once. Her glance flicked over Amy disdainfully.

'Won't you introduce me to this charming child?' she purred sweetly.

She was clever, thought Amy, and bitchy. Her subtle emphasis on the word 'child' had effectively isolated Amy, making her the intruder. She suddenly felt very young and gauche. She was no match for this woman. Matt, however, apart from a slight tightening of his mouth, seemed not to have noticed, as he introduced them with urbane politeness.

'Amy, Celine Rousseau. Celine, Amy Lawrence. Do excuse us, Celine, I have to talk to Amy.' Taking Amy's arm, he steered her across the room. She could feel Celine Rousseau's malicious eyes boring into her back as they walked, and she shook free of Matt's grip, still angry.

'What do you want to talk to me about?' she asked with flashing eyes.

'Good God, Amy, what's the matter with you?' Irritation laced his voice as he stared down at her darkly.

'Nothing. I just thought that you'd want to make it quick, so you could get back to your friend,' she replied waspishly.

An enlightened smile curved Matt's firm mouth, the irritation leaving his face.

'Ah, you're jealous, sweet Amy,' he murmured triumphantly.

'I am not!' she snapped, feeling the urge to slap that mocking, knowing smile from his face. 'If you prefer the company of that ... that ... horrible woman to mine, then that's fine by me.' Suddenly the whole thing seemed too absurd, and laughter rose inside her like a bubble.

'Yes, I am jealous,' she admitted grudgingly, a smile playing at the corners of her mouth. 'She had her arms round you.'

'Not for long, my love. Celine is a bitch—she does it for effect. I don't know who she came with, I certainly didn't invite her. God, I thought you'd never get here—I've been waiting and waiting for you— falling prey to the likes of Celine,' he murmured wickedly, passing her a glass. 'Drink,' he ordered. smiling down at her. 'How could you think that I would have anything to do with Celine?' he went on. 'You know that you're the only woman I care for—and you look exquisite tonight, the most beautiful woman in the place. I want you,' he whispered, for her ears alone.

Having made his peace with her, the misunderstanding between them sorted out, he kept her
at his side for the rest of the evening, his arm around
her shoulder for a great deal of the time. Amy caught
Celine's hard eyes on them more than once. She was
obviously infatuated with Matt, and Amy felt a little
sorry for her.

John Wilson joined them later in the evening.
'You two are getting on well,' he remarked, a specu-
lative look on his face.

Matt lifted Amy's hand to his lips. 'I find your
assistant dazzling,' he replied, pressing his mouth to
her palm.

The party went well, and Matt's sculptures were
unanimously praised. They were beautiful, thought
Amy, letting her hands slide over the smooth dark
wood of her particular favourite. It was a large ab-
stract composition in wood and bronze that fascinated her. It had an age-old theme, Mother and
Child, and the shapes were rounded and sensual. It
was not for sale, even though she could not have
afforded it anyway. Glancing around the exhibition,
she saw that a number of the pieces had been sold
that evening, on the understanding that they
remain in the gallery, until the end of the exhibition.
She was glad. Matt deserved success, even if he did
not particularly crave it.

Turning away, she decided to visit the ladies'
room before they left. She was just powdering her
nose, which had gone a little shiny as usual, when
Celine entered, and not by chance, Amy was sure.

'Amy, my dear, I want a little chat with you,' she
began silkily, eyeing her perfect reflection with satisfaction.

'I don't think we have anything to say to each
other,' Amy replied evenly, hoping that the other

woman was not going to make a scene.

'Oh, but I think we have.' Celine's eyes hardened, making her face look tight and unattractive. 'How long have you known Matt?' she asked, looking at Amy disdainfully.

'About three weeks, but I don't really see that it's any of your business.' Amy's voice sounded calm, but she was beginning to feel a faint stirring of anger at Celine's personal questions.

Celine's eyes flashed, but her tone was still silky. 'It is my business. You see, Matt and I are . . . how shall I put it? . . . very close friends.'

Amy bristled at this. 'Well, if you're such close friends, I'm surprised Matt hasn't told you himself how long we've known each other,' she retorted, sweetly sarcastic.

She did not want to stand there trading insults with Celine, she thought wearily. It had been a long tiring day, and she was no match for this woman.

Celine was eyeing her with open distaste now, her expression malicious. 'Well, of course, Matt is a very virile man. I expect he needs a little diversion now and again, especially with his wife being away such a lot. But I really didn't think that a mousey little thing like you would catch his attention. How *did* you do it?' Her tone was deliberately insulting, and Amy flinched away from the narrowed catlike stare, that was sliding insolently over her.

Two words were pounding in her head. 'His wife?' she echoed weakly, a sudden attack of faintness making her sway against the wall.

Celine's laugh was brittle. 'He didn't tell you he was married?' A cruel smile curved her full mouth. 'Isn't that just like him? Of course he's married. You didn't expect a man like that to be free, did you?' She laughed again, mocking Amy's stupidity in no uncertain terms, derision in her eyes. 'Yes, Joanne, his wife, is in New York at the moment, she's been there for about four months. She looks a little like you, actually. Although she's much more attractive.' Supremely aware as she was of Amy's pale face and wild, hurt eyes, Celine's smile was triumphant and sadistically smug.

'You really are a fool. It must have made a change for Matt to have somebody like you in his bed. You have been to bed with him, I suppose. He wouldn't be bothering with you otherwise. I'd tidy myself up if I were you, you look a mess.'

Amy was holding herself rigid, willing herself with every last ounce of her self-control not to break down. She had nothing to say to Celine, although she would have given anything at that moment to be cool and bitchy back, to appear unmoved by the other woman's malicious remarks.

Casually flicking back a glossy auburn curl, Celine delivered her parting shot. 'I mustn't keep Matt waiting. From what he tells me, I think he needs someone with a little more experience than you tonight.' With her long curved body swaying seductively, she left the room.

Amy collapsed on one of the small, ornate stools as soon as she had gone, still feeling faint. In the past five minutes her life had been torn apart. Matt Cavanagh was married, and for all Amy knew, he might well have children.

Her face burned with humiliation, and she buried her head in her hands, remembering how she had flung herself at him. Hot tears scorched down her face. She could not blame him, she had sensed his withdrawal from the start, and she had refused to accept it. She had wanted him, and despite his gentle rejection, had forced herself on him. She would never be able to look him in the face again. Misery engulfed her, as, thinking back over the time they had spent together, she realised that not once, even at the height of their lovemaking, had he said he loved her. He had not mentioned love at all, it was she who had constantly told him of her love. How he must have laughed!

As Celine had said, why should she have thought that a man like Matt would be free? He was thirty, after all, and exceptionally attractive in every way. He had his pick of women, and Amy, wanting to believe it, had stupidly imagined that she was his choice. He had asked her to marry him, probably to make her feel better after what she had done. She cringed as she thought of the way she had practically solicited him for sex. And it was no wonder, her thoughts ran wildly on, that he had taken her to Crete. He would not want any of his friends or business associates to see him with a woman who was not his wife, around London.

Oh God, what could she do?

Flaying herself with shame, she turned her thoughts to Matt's behaviour. In a way he had tricked her, she thought angrily, wanting him to share some of the guilt. He had never mentioned his wife, he had acted as though he was a free man.

Joanne. The name ran through her head. She had always despised women who came between man and wife, seeing no excuse for their behaviour, and now here she was, one of them. She had to get away from London; she would not see Matt again.

Slowly her tears dried, and, weary with misery, she stood up and examined her ravaged face in the mirror. Her eyes were red and swollen, her eye make-up streaked all over her face.

She pulled the flowers from her hair viciously,

hardly noticing the pain, and bathed her face, splashing plenty of cold water on her eyes, hoping to reduce the swelling. Drying her face, she found that she looked a lot better.

She intended to leave the party immediately; she could not stay a moment longer. She brushed her hair and smoothed down her dress, her mechanical actions somehow soothing. Then keeping her head down, she opened the door and walked out.

Matt was standing just outside, waiting for her. Amy closed her eyes tiredly. Even now, with all she knew, her heart was beating painfully fast at the sight of him. He turned towards her, concern in his eyes as he noticed her ravaged face, and wild, hurt expression.

'Amy, what in God's name have you been doing in there? I've been standing here for half an hour. What's the matter?' He shook her slightly as he spoke.

She shrugged out of his grasp. 'Leave me alone!' she spat, her voice low and hostile. 'I'm sure Celine is waiting for you!'

She walked away quickly, pushing her way through the crowd to collect her wrap, knowing that he was watching her, astonished.

She looked back once more as she left the gallery. I just want to see his face one more time, she told herself desperately, and to her horror she saw him pushing his way through, towards her.

Turning on her heel, she ran, hailing a taxi as she went, needing to get away.

She didn't realise she was holding her breath until the taxi moved off, in response to her trembling instructions, and she let out a long weak sigh. Peering through the back window, she saw Matt running out of the gallery, and stopping in the middle of the road. He stared after her, his face grim and angry.

Arriving back at the flat, she was still trembling, her thoughts desolate and despairing. Not bothering to switch on any lights, she sat in the dark, staring at nothing, with wide hurt eyes. For once she was glad that Joni was away, and she was alone.

Suddenly the door bell rang, and Amy shrank back into her seat. It was Matt. She was not going to let him in. He rang again, and she put her hands over her ears, praying that he would go away. Then she heard him banging on the flat door. He had managed to get through the front door of the house.

'Let me in, Amy,' his voice was quiet, but determined. 'Let me in, or I'll break this door down.'

He wouldn't, she thought dully, but was proved wrong as she heard his shoulder hitting the door. She stood up angrily. Who did he think he was, trying to force entry into her flat, when she did not want to see him? His shoulder thudded against the door for a second time, and she walked over to let him in. He was going to get in anyway, and she might as well not have the added expense of a new lock. She might have known that she could not get away from him so easily.

He walked into the flat slowly, gracefully, his face a mask of rage.

'How did you get past the front door? Did you break that down as well?' She faced him angrily, feeling repulsion at the sight of his strongly moulded face.

He spoke through his teeth, his temper barely controlled. 'I rang upstairs, and told them that your bell wasn't working. They let me in.'

'You devious swine!' she choked. 'Get out of here now, before I call the police!'

'You won't be calling the police, my love. You're

going to listen to what I've got to say to you.' He took a step towards her, and she flinched away.

'Where's Celine? Waiting outside in the car?' she taunted sarcastically. 'She won't take kindly to this interruption of her evening.'

Matt's fingers closed on her shoulders and he shook her hard, his eyes as cold as ice.

'Be quiet!' he hissed. 'Why did you run out on me at the gallery?'

'I wanted to get away from you. You're a liar and a cheat, and I never, *never* want to see you again. Do you hear me?' she shouted, anger throbbing through her body at what he had destroyed in her. 'You don't deny that you're married I suppose!' she spat at him.

Arrogance lifted Matt's head, his gaze suddenly coldly mocking as he looked at her. 'No, I don't deny it. I am married.' His statement was clear, and flatly spoken, and Amy died a little inside. His jaw tightened as she lashed out at him, delivering a stinging blow across his face.

He grabbed her arms, twisting them behind her back. She watched with clinical interest, as the red mark on his face faded.

'You go too far, Amy,' he grated, still keeping a barely-controlled rein on his temper, his eyes glittering between the heavy lids. But Amy was past caring, blind with rage, as she struggled in his merciless grip.

'You bastard! You deceived me, letting me believe that you wanted me ...'

He cut across her heated words, a smile curving his mouth, that did not reach his hard eyes.

'Such language,' he drawled coolly. 'And let me remind you, it was you who wanted me. Did you expect me to turn down what was so charmingly offered?'

She was speechless with anger, but inside she was crying. His cruel remark had cut home like a knife.

Matt continued, his voice ice-cold, 'And you still want me, just as much as I want you.'

'I don't want you, I hate you!' but even as she screamed at him, she could feel desire, shivering treacherously along her veins, making a liar of her. I don't want him, she repeated to herself silently, trying to make it true, praying that she could resist him if he tried to make love to her.

He was so cruel, deliberately reminding her of what she had offered in love. Taunting her coldly, with the one thing she would regret all her life.

'If you touch me,' she gritted, 'I'll lay charges against you for rape!' Her eyes were wild and hysterical, as she battled inwardly with hatred and desire. How could her body turn traitor on her now?

'Oh no, you won't, sweet Amy, because it won't be rape.' His voice was quiet and dangerous.

His mouth was descending slowly, his narrowed eyes glinting savagely, as he watched her twisting futilely in his grip.

'I hate you,' she moaned again, as if repeating the words could make them true.

'Little liar.' His breath was hot against her face as he spoke. Then his mouth came down on hers, punishing and cruel. Her lips were ground against her teeth, and his hold on her arms did not slacken. They were still twisted behind her back, and he used his strength to arch her body against him. The deliberately slow exploration of her mouth was weakening her resistance, wringing an unwilling response from her. Desire that she despised, flooded through her, rising like a boiling tide. She felt so weary and hurt, and the knowledge that resistance was futile closed her eyes heavily, and her control snapped as her mouth parted beneath his.

His vice-like grip on her arms loosened then, his hands slid over her body in the familiar, intimate pattern that made her moan softly, as he cupped her breasts possessively. He kissed her mouth deeply, gently, and she could not fight him any more. She wanted him, needed him, and the abandon that his caresses were inducing was too sweet for her to deny him.

He lifted her into his arms, his molten eyes scanning the softness of her parted lips. His voice was low and husky with desire.

'You're mine, Amy,' he said, and she could not argue. She did not want to. He had enforced his ownership so positively, with every kiss, with every touch of his hard sculptor's hands, that she knew it was true. She was urgent with desire, aware that it was deliberately induced, but uncaring as he carried her to the bedroom. And then they were on her bed, Matt's hands suddenly urgent as he eased her beneath him gently. His lips were at her throat, and she wound her arms around his neck, her response to his fierce and passionate advances absolute.

'Love me, Matt,' she whispered desperately, running her hands feverishly over his bare brown chest. But as if her words brought him to his senses, he stiffened immediately, and with one lithe, graceful movement he jerked away from her almost roughly, leaving her suddenly cold and alone, as she stared at him confusedly. He was fighting to gain control as he lay beside her, and even as she watched, iron self-control stiffened his body, holding him stiff and tense, his hands clenched into fists at his sides. He had rejected her, and despite herself, Amy began to cry, long shuddering sobs tearing her body. She felt sick with shame at her own weakness, at the unfulfilled desire that was aching inside her.

Matt turned to her. 'Oh God, Amy . . .' he groaned, his voice shaken and low. 'It can't be like this between us . . . not in anger . . . forgive me . . .'

He tried to comfort her, his eyes bleak with distress, but she pulled away from him, refusing the reassuring warmth and security that his arms offered, and buried her face in the pillow. She still loved him—that was the worst part of it—but she did not have to listen to his excuses.

She heard him get out of bed. He was silent as he dressed. He was going to leave, and she was too weary to stop him. She needed to talk to him, but the words would not come, so she buried her face deeper into the pillow, as he left the room.

Ten minutes later he returned. He placed his hand gently on her shoulder and she flinched involuntarily, sensing his anger at her fear. She turned to look at him when it became apparent that he was not going to move. He was standing over her, tall and virile, his waistcoat still unbuttoned, watchfully scanning her white, tear-stained face, a defeated sorrow, and self-disgust evident in his unveiled eyes.

'Tea,' he said quietly, holding out a cup. 'Amy, I . . .'

He got no farther. Amy reached up and knocked the cup from his hand, blind rage dictating her actions. Bringing her tea, she thought wildly, as if that could make anything better!

'Go away and leave me alone. I don't want your stupid tea. I just want you to go!' she screamed at him.

Matt watched the cup roll across the carpet, the tea sinking slowly into the thick pile, spreading into an ugly stain, and his mouth compressed tightly.

Concern left his dark eyes, to be replaced with cold anger, and an almost desperate misery, that closed his face. He turned and left the room, without a word, and she heard the front door slam violently.

'Matt,' she whispered achingly, as a fresh torrent of tears began oozing out of her eyes.

But he was gone.

CHAPTER SIX

AMY finally got out of bed at dawn. She had not slept at all; her mind was too active with chaotic, jumbled thoughts.

She took a hot shower, scrubbing herself thoroughly, and then drank three cups of strong black coffee, hoping that it would clear her head. She paced the flat, smoking heavily, as she decided what to do. She had to get away from London. But where could she go?

She would not be Matt's mistress. He would not use her again, as he had last night, because she was not going to give him the chance. If she was not going to give him the chance, she had to get away— immediately. She despised herself for the way he could affect her. He only had to look at her with those dark, molten eyes, and desire clawed inside her, like a caged animal desperate for release. It would have been so easy if she did not love him, she thought despairingly.

It was then that the idea came to her. She would go to Cornwall. He would never find here there, even if he bothered to look. She picked up the phone eagerly, and put it down again, realising the early hour. Her grandfather would not be up yet, but she could pack her things now.

She walked purposefully into the bedroom and pulled her cases down from the top of the wardrobe. She packed all her clothes, tidily and slowly, her mind ice-calm as she worked. Also in the cases she packed a few of her personal possessions from around the flat. She was not really bothered about the rest of her things. Perhaps Joni could have them sent on to Cornwall later. It did not matter.

Glancing at the clock, she saw that it was after eight. She would ring John Wilson at exactly nine, and in the meantime she would write a note to Joni. It was brief and to the point, explaining that she and Matt were finished, and needing to get away, she was going to Cornwall for a while. Adding that she would phone as soon as Joni got back, she specifically requested Joni not to give Matt any information about her, should he ask. Signing it, she left it in a prominent position on the table. She then rang Paddington Station to find out train times to Cornwall, noting them down carefully on a pad by the phone. She was amazed at how cool she felt. Drained and empty, the pain and humiliation had become unbearable, so she had detached herself from it, in a strange way. Later, it would hurt like hell, but at the moment she felt nothing but sheer indifference.

She made some more coffee, and smoked a cigarette slowly as she drank. It was nine o'clock, time to ring John. She picked up the receiver and dialled the gallery, and John answered.

'John, it's Amy. I'm sorry, but I'll have to ask for some time off—leave of absence. A relative of mine has died, and I have to travel to Scotland.' She hated lying to him, and felt cheap and mean for deceiving him, but she had no choice. She would write later, and explain that she would not be back, but just now she needed an excuse that would make the conversation short.

Noting the quiet grief in her almost expressionless voice, John agreed immediately.

'Of course, Amy, take as long as you need. Just phone me when you want to come back. I'm very sorry.' He was sweet and sympathetic, and Amy had to fight back tears as she rang off.

How she hated herself. Lying, and running out on people who trusted her. Three weeks ago she had been an ordinary girl, living her uneventful life happily. Now she was in flight, the mistress of a married man. A man she loved with all her heart. A man who did not return her love, and had deceived her.

Pulling herself together, she went to the bedroom to dress. Although the weather was fairly mild, she felt bitterly cold. She shrugged into black trousers and tucked them into knee-length black boots. She slipped a black tee-shirt over her head and began brushing out her hair. It was tousled, and full of knots where Matt had run his fingers through it so urgently. She twisted it into a neat chignon, deciding to get it cut as soon as she got to Cornwall. It would be easier to manage, and she wanted nothing to remind her of Matt. Pulling on a short sheepskin jacket, she carried her cases into the hall, checking her appearance in the mirror, as she dialled for a taxi. Her eyes were haunted, deep dark shadows beneath, making them huge in her pale, drawn face, but she could not be bothered with make-up. The urge to get away was strong, the sooner the better, and she did not want to waste time trying to make herself look as if her heart wasn't broken.

With the taxi due to arrive in fifteen minutes, Amy collected her handbag from the bedroom, checking that it contained everything she needed, and closed the door for the last time. She wandered through all the other rooms, shutting the doors behind her, silently saying goodbye. She had spent happy times here with Joni, but too much had happened to allow her to stay.

The phone rang as she was washing her coffee cup. It was Matt. She knew instinctively, so she did not answer it. The moment it stopped ringing, she snatched up the receiver and dialled her grandfather's number. It rang for some time before it was answered, but finally she heard his kind old voice asking suspiciously who was on the other end.

'Granddad, it's me, Amy. How are you?'

'Amy!' His voice was pleased. 'I'm fine, lass, how are you? This is an early call, is anything wrong?'

'Not really, but could I come down and stay with you for a while?' Her voice was pleading, and her grandfather responded immediately.

'Of course, love. You know I'll be as pleased as Punch to see you. Are you coming today?'

'Yes, I'll be there this afternoon. I'll explain then.' The doorbell rang. 'There's my taxi, I'll have to go. See you later, Granddad, goodbye!' She slammed down the receiver and rushed to the front door. The phone began ringing again, and an uncharacteristically cruel smile curved Amy's lips. Matt could call as much as he liked, but he would never see her again. She could not see what his problem was. Celine was more than willing to step into her shoes. She scathingly imagined that it must be his fragile male pride, unwilling to admit that he had lost her.

The cab driver put her cases in the trunk and she took one last look around the flat, before slamming the front door for the final time. The taxi was just turning on to the main road, when she saw Matt's car driving towards them. Her breath caught in her throat as he passed, and she crouched in her seat, horror-stricken, praying that he would not see her. She peeped out of the window, to see him turning into her road. Letting out a long sigh of pure relief, she sat up again. Nonetheless she did not feel safe until the train pulled out of the station and numerous glances over her shoulder had satisfied her that Matt was not on the train. She felt like a fugitive. His persistence surprised her a little. She imagined him hammering on the front door of the flat, unwilling to believe that she was not there, and giggled. Then he would go to the gallery. She hoped he suffered.

The train journey was long, and although Amy enjoyed looking at the countryside, it became boring. There was something rhythmic and soothing about the motion of the train, and drained by lack of sleep, she soon fell asleep.

She awoke some time later to find herself being shaken by the woman in the next seat. She woke in panic, imagining that Matt had found her, to find the woman staring at her worriedly. Amy had asked her to wake her if she was still asleep at her station.

'Next one's yours, dear,' she said kindly. 'You look worn out, you poor child,' she added.

Smiling and murmuring a non-committal reply, Amy thanked her, and pulled her cases out of the luggage rack.

As she stepped off the train, and on to the country platform, she felt relieved and absurdly free. The sun was shining brightly, and the birds were making a terrific din. Later, the distance between her and Matt would be almost too much to bear, but now it was perfect. She walked to her grandfather's house, hardly noticing the weight of her two heavy suitcases. Her grandfather came to the door to greet her when she arrived, his pleasure at seeing her touching. He took her cases and made her sit down. He made a pot of tea, and sliced the cake that he had bought especially from the village, and brought them in on a tray, spread with a clean cloth.

It was too much for Amy, and she jumped to her feet, flinging her arms around him.

'Oh, Granddad, I love you,' she whispered. 'Thanks for being so kind and understanding,' and so saying, she burst into tears, the strain and pressure of the last twenty-four hours suddenly unbearable. Sam Lawrence held her tightly, not prying, knowing that she would tell him what was wrong when she was ready. Amy cried until she had no more tears left, then sat down, pale and shaking, thankfully sipping the hot tea that her grandfather pressed into her hands.

'I'm sorry,' she whispered.

'Don't apologise, lass. I know something's badly wrong, but it seems to me that what you need is a good rest—you're exhausted. I'll take your cases upstairs, and when you've finished that tea you can go and rest till teatime. Then if you're feeling any better and you want to talk, we will.' He smiled at her understandingly.

'Thanks, Granddad, I am very tired,' she replied wearily.

She finished her tea, and followed him upstairs, her feet dragging heavily. He had drawn the curtains in the pretty floral room and to Amy's tired glance it looked like a haven of peace and comfort. 'You rest now, Amy. I'll see you later.' Her grandfather left the room quietly. She would never be able to thank him enough for what he had done for her.

She kicked off her boots, lay down on the soft bed, and was asleep within minutes. She slept for long dreamless hours, until her grandfather woke her up for supper. She stumbled downstairs, still sleepy, and ate a fair amount of the delicious beef stew that her grandfather had prepared. She had not eaten for twenty-four hours, but strangely she was not hungry.

However, she forced herself to do justice to the meal, knowing the trouble that had gone into it.

After a number of steaming cups of refreshing, fragrant tea, they sat in front of the crackling log fire, and Amy knew that the time had come to explain why she had come to Cornwall, She did not want to think back, the pain was still too fresh, so she was brief, skipping over many important details. But with her grandfather's shrewd eyes upon her, she guessed that by her stumbling words and long silences she gave herself away.

Sam Lawrence did not judge or criticise her actions, but comforted her gently, when the tears that she could not control slid sadly down her face, assuring her that she could stay with him for as long as she wanted. Soon after, blessing his understanding, she went back to bed, sleeping deeply until well after noon the next day.

Gradually her life in Cornwall fell into a gentle pattern. It was not easy, and sometimes Amy felt like running back to London, to give herself to Matt, whatever his terms. Her days were filled with thoughts of him, and her nights haunted by dreams of him.

She often saw pictures of him in the newspapers; his reputation was spreading, and she would stare for hours at the awful grainy pictures, her heart aching with longing to know how he was. He never got in touch with her, never attempted to find out where she was, and unreasonably perhaps, Amy felt hurt and lonely. It was proof, if she had needed any, that he had never loved her.

She went over every minute they had spent together carefully, as if looking for some clue to what went wrong. She grew thin and ill, love becoming a disease that ravaged her slender frame. It was during that time, when she felt too weak to leave her bed, that her mind began to clear. The summer had slipped by unnoticed, she thought, as she gazed out of the window at the autumn landscape, and the realisation piqued her. This one positive thought set her on the road to recovery. She began to eat sensibly, forcing her thoughts away from Matt Cavanagh, and soon she was well again, although her scars never really healed.

She advertised in shop windows in the village, and began to take in typing, book-keeping and other clerical work. She filled her days cleaning the cottage, shopping, and taking long walks along the stark Cornish cliffs. Slowly, she built up her life again, making the adjustment to life without Matt, and she felt proud and strong. Until now.

The words echoed round her aching head as she returned to the present. Glancing up, she saw that it had gone dark while she had been sitting there, lost in the past. The past that she had managed to put behind her after a long and painful struggle. Why had Matt come here? Not that his reason really mattered, his presence was enough to knock her off balance, and that was how she felt—disturbed and uneasy, as she went to bed.

CHAPTER SEVEN

AFTER a troubled night, Amy awoke early next morning. Dreams that she had not experienced for years had haunted her sleep. She had a busy day ahead of her, so she was glad of the early start. Dressing quickly, after a cool shower, in olive green corduroy trousers and a thin white cheesecloth smock, she dragged back her thick hair into a pony-tail and ran downstairs to start work.

It was such a beautiful morning that she decided to go for a swim after she had finished the morning chores. She took her grandfather a cup of tea, then set about preparing breakfast. The appetising smell of frying bacon filled the kitchen, but Amy felt slightly sickened by it, nibbling only a small piece of toast, and drinking four cups of strong coffee, for her morning meal.

After breakfast she washed the dishes and began making the weekly bread. She was unusually violent with the dough, imagining that it was Matt Cavanagh, and punching it into submission.

Two hours later the cottage was filled with the delicious aroma of freshly baked bread, and Amy made the beds briskly, before sitting down with a mid-morning cup of tea.

She had a couple of spare hours before lunchtime, now that the bread was baked, so she rushed upstairs and changed into her bikini, putting her clothes back on over it. The urge to go for a swim was so strong that she gave in to it, so grabbing a large beach towel, she slammed the front door and walked towards the sea.

She had found a small sandy cove that was always deserted owing to its inaccessibility. A steep rocky path led down to it, so steep that even Amy stumbled a good many times, sending showers of tiny pebbles down to the beach below. She knew that the path was unsafe and dangerous, but she enjoyed the solitude of the deserted beach so much that she considered the difficulty worth it.

Once on the beach, she stripped off her clothes quickly, and leaving them on top of a safe rock, ran into the water. It was freezing, and she gasped as she plunged in. Swimming strongly, she made her way towards an outjutting rock, and reaching it, climbed up to the top and sat down, short of breath. The strong sun soon dried her wet, salty skin, and she shook out her black hair and gazed out to sea. She came here often, always enjoying the warmth and solitude.

Turning towards the beach, her gaze suddenly fell on the tall figure of a man, standing quite still, his head turned towards her.

Matt Cavanagh, she thought, her mouth going dry. Invading her privacy again. He must have followed her, because nobody ever came to this beach except her. Angry and frightened she turned back towards the sea. Perhaps if she ignored him he would go away. She lifted her face to the sun. She would stay here until he had gone. She wanted nothing to do with him.

A few moments later he pulled himself on to the rock. Amy turned towards him furiously, her words sticking in her throat as she looked at him. In only brief black swimming trunks, the hard male strength of him made her senses reel. Water dripped from his smooth-skinned body, his muscles rippling as he levered himself into a comfortable position.

'Go away,' she said clearly, her eyes fixed on his powerful brown shoulders. He did not move or speak, and she forced herself to look up into his face, and as she met his dark eyes, her heart lurched sickeningly. His steady gaze was fixed on her face, but slowly it slid appraisingly down her body as she watched, taking in the skimpy yellow bikini that barely covered any part of her curved slender shape. His glance was almost an intimate caress, on her full breasts, slim waist and long brown legs. She gritted her teeth under his intense scrutiny, fighting the urge to cover herself. She could feel her body responding shamelessly to his almost physical glance. Slowly his gaze returned to her face, noting the angry strain on it, and he smiled, a mocking, cynical smile that did not reach his glittering eyes.

'You're just as beautiful as I remember,' he said coolly, mocking the modesty that made her want to cover herself. He missed nothing.

'Why have you come here?' she demanded, trying to take her mind off the way she was feeling inside.

'I have business here,' he answered smoothly, his eyes narrowed and unreadable against the glare of the sun.

She wondered what business he could possibly have in this small Cornish village, but she did not ask. She would not give him the satisfaction of knowing how curious she was. She wanted him to go away. 'How's your wife?' she asked calmly, hoping that her question might get rid of him.

His mouth compressed angrily. 'Fine, I imagine,' he replied grimly.

'You neglect her.' Hurt by his cool arrogance and obvious irritation with her, Amy was angry and uncaring in her choice of words, wanting to hurt him, as she turned on him, her eyes flashing gold. 'Sleeping around when she's away. I feel sorry for her, having such an unfaithful husband.' Her words were clearly spoken, and she heard his angry intake of breath with a strange pleasure.

Matt grabbed her arm, twisting it behind her back. 'You little bitch!' he grated furiously. 'You know nothing about it.' His eyes were cold and angry, and Amy's breasts heaved with fear.

'Matt, let me go. You're hurting me,' she whispered wearily, all the fight gone from her.

He let go of her immediately. 'You shouldn't be so damned rude, if you don't want to take the consequences,' he said unpleasantly.

Feeling really frightened, Amy slid into the water, and swam strongly for the shore. Matt did not follow her, so she turned suspiciously and saw him still sitting on the rock, gazing out to sea. Sadly, she saw the tiredness about him that she had not noticed before.

Suddenly an agonising pain shot through her leg, and she could not move. She sank into the water, paralysed with agony, feeling it closing over her head, and she panicked. Sea water was filling her mouth and nose and she could not breathe. She was going to drown. Her heart was pounding, as she tried to thrash her way to the surface, choking. She called Matt's name with all her remaining strength, as the water closed over her head once more. Her leg still would not move, arrows of burning pain were shooting through her body. She stopped struggling, wearily. It was a waste of effort.

Then Matt was beside her, pulling her head out of the water, guiding her to the shore, saving her life. She clung to his wet body, retching. When the water became shallow enough for him to stand in, he swung her into his arms and carried her up the beach, laying her gently down on the soft sand. He knelt beside her, massaging the locked muscle of her leg with strong fingers. She felt sick and very weak, and she could see that he was still angry with her.

'Matt . . .' she began weakly.

'You little fool,' he grated, his cold glance pinning her down mercilessly. 'You nearly drowned! Don't come here again alone.' She turned her head away, flinching from his anger, tears squeezing between her tightly closed eyelids.

His voice softened at her distress. 'Amy, don't cry,' he murmured, and with a muffled epithet he pulled her into his arms, pressing her head against the cool damp skin of his broad chest. He smoothed her heavy wet hair away from her face with gentle hands. She could not stop crying. Relief that she had not drowned, and the disappearance of his anger made her sob like a baby for long minutes.

He held her tightly, letting her cry, knowing that she needed the release, until finally she lifted her head.

'I'm sorry,' she whispered, sniffing loudly. 'You saved my life.'

Matt smiled, his dark eyes intent as they rested on her mouth. 'You shouldn't swim out so far alone. Promise me that you won't in future.'

'I promise,' she replied, rubbing away her tears with shaking fingers. Matt leaned forward, pressing his mouth to her hot, swollen eyelids. His touch was like cool balm, and she swayed against him, unable to stop herself.

'Matt . . .' his name parted her lips as he claimed them hungrily, kissing her deeply, as his arms tightened around her.

The old fever burst between them, making them cling tightly together. His hands slid to the naked skin of her waist, fondling her, slowly. She wanted to give in to him. She was waiting to be back in his arms, caressed by his lean powerful hands, kissed by his hard, sensual mouth, possessed by him. The desire between them would never be assuaged. As far as their urgent bodies were concerned, three years had passed into nothing. They could never get enough of each other.

A seagull screeching loudly overhead brought Amy to her senses and she pulled out of Matt's arms, shuddering, her eyes brilliant, her face flushed. Standing up, she burst out bitterly, 'How dare you! Don't touch me again. If you think that I'm going to be your mistress, you're sadly mistaken. I won't be used, Matt, I'm not a stupid young teenager any more. Go back to your wife!' She turned away, trembling, still weak with unfulfilled desire, and gathered up her clothes.

He did not move, but his mouth twisted viciously as he replied. 'You can't deny that you want me, Amy. You will be my lover again, because you can't say no,' he taunted. 'The disgust and outrage that you pretend to feel soon fades when I have you in my arms.' She flinched at his hurtful words. His expression was openly cynical, as his eyes slid over her body insolently.

'You're mine. Don't forget that.'

Amy stared at him, shocked. He was possessive and ruthless, and he would never let her go. She hated him at that moment.

'I'm not yours,' she spat, repulsed by his obsession with ownership. 'I belong to nobody but myself.'

He smiled humourlessly, his eyes grim. 'We'll see,' was all he said, his voice remote and faintly bored as he reached for his cigarettes.

He had dismissed her. Seething with rage, she opened her mouth to tell him exactly what she thought of him, then shut it abruptly. Better to go home and get away from him. Making him angry would only rebound on her, distressingly. Swallowing back her angry retort with difficulty, she strode stiffly towards the steep path. She was in flight from him, and they both knew it, and she did not look back as she stumbled upwards, hurt pride stiffening her spine.

Matt was so damned sure of himself, she fumed impotently. She would never be his lover again. Love was not a game, and he was not the winner. Just because he had saved her life, he expected her to melt into his arms. His tenacious arrogance appalled her. Why didn't he leave her alone?

Sighing, she reached the top of the cliff. If she was honest, she realised miserably, she did want him, but not on his terms, and she would keep out of his way in future.

She had just finished putting away the lunch dishes when the telephone rang. Despite the events of the morning, Amy's heart began to pound and her fingers shook as she lifted the receiver, wanting it to be Matt on the other end, and praying that it wasn't. It was Howard Jordan.

'Amy? Is that you?'

Filled with irritating disappointment, Amy realised that she had not spoken since picking up the phone.

'Hello, Howard, how are you?'

'I'm fine. Is something wrong? Are you ill?'

Shamed by the concern in his voice, Amy made an effort to pull herself together. 'No—no, everything is fine. Really.'

'Will you come out to dinner with me this week?'
His low voice was persuasive.

'Yes, I'd love to,' she replied. Not strictly true, of
course, but it would take her mind off Matt—she
hoped.

'When?'

She could hear the smile in his voice, and was
disgusted with herself for using him.

'The day after tomorrow?'

'That would be fine. I'm looking forward to seeing
you. Shall I pick you up about seven-thirty?'

'Yes. Howard . . .?' Not really knowing what she
wanted to say, Amy trailed off weakly.

'Yes?'

'Nothing—I'm sorry. I'll see you on Friday . . .
Goodbye.'

She put down the receiver hurriedly, wondering
at her own motives. Howard Jordan was very fond
of her, and he was an easy and undemanding companion, tall and blond with cool grey eyes. She had
let him take her out at first, because he was, in every
way, the exact opposite to Matt. Gradually friendship had grown between them—nothing more on
Amy's part. Even the knowledge that Howard loved
her and was hoping to marry her could not unfreeze
the coldness around her heart, and apart from a
chaste kiss on the cheek every now and then, she
could not let him touch her. Matt was the only man
she had ever desired. Angry that her thoughts were
always of him, she decided to do some work.

She spent the rest of the afternoon typing a
number of business letters for a friend of her grandfather. The work was still not finished by dinner
time, because try as she might she could not put
Matt out of her thoughts. Half way through the
mouthwatering baked fish, her grandfather looked

up at her worriedly. She returned his glance, wondering what was wrong.

'Granddad, you've been looking at me like that ever since we sat down. What's the matter?' Her smile as she spoke softened the exasperation in her voice.

Sam Lawrence shook his head. 'Well, lass, I suppose I'd better tell you. I've asked Matt Cavanagh over for dinner tomorrow.'

'You've done what?' Her voice was high, her face astonished. 'I don't believe you!'

'Well, it's true, Amy love. I met him this afternoon, in the village, and we got talking—we had quite a long chat, and I got the impression that— well, that he's not looking after himself, not eating properly. There's no electricity at Old Farm Cottage, you know, and it's only common decency to help a neighbour out . . .' His voice trailed off at the look of horror on Amy's face.

'Granddad,' she wailed, 'how could you?'

'Amy, you've got to face him. It's been three years since you left him. You can't pretend that he doesn't exist, especially with him living just down the lane.'

Her grandfather was earnest and she knew that he was right, but she had not told him about her two encounters with Matt. She had tried to face him and come off worst.

'I know you're right, Granddad, but I can't, I just can't.' She was upset, the thought of Matt coming to the cottage for dinner made her feel ill.

'You can, Amy, and you will,' her grandfather's voice was firm and soothing. 'You can't run away for ever, love.'

Amy sighed. She knew that he was doing his best, but he did not know the true situation. She began to explain, but he cut across her. 'Amy, do it for me.

You're not a child any more. You're twenty-one years old. You ran away three years ago, are you going to run away all your life?'

If I have to, she thought miserably. Her grandfather was pleading with her, and in her heart she knew that he was right. She would go through with it for his sake. He was only trying to help, after all.

'Very well, I'll do it for you,' she murmured grudgingly.

'I'm proud of you, Amy.' Her grandfather's face was wreathed with smiles. 'I told him dinner at seven-thirty, will that be all right?'

'Yes. I'll cook something special as he's starving to death at Old Farm Cottage.'

Her smiling sarcasm was lost on her grandfather. She was angry because she suspected Matt of being behind this. He had probably wormed his way round her grandfather, for the dinner invitation.

Pretending that he could not cook. She knew very well that he could. Using his undoubted charm to trick her grandfather into becoming involved in their private struggle was despicable. She felt like poisoning his food. She would be cool and remote; he could not touch her in front of her grandfather, she hoped.

Later that evening, Amy decided what she would serve for dinner the next day. Her final choice was steak—steak that she knew Matt could cook, although she realised that the idea of shaming him was ridiculous. He was always in control of every situation, his innate charm and self-assurance saw to that.

Sighing, she went upstairs to shower before retiring to bed. Once she was in bed, though, she could not sleep. She tossed and turned, her thoughts disturbed. It was all very well for her grandfather to advise her not to run away, but what else could she do? Matt Cavanagh was not a man to give up easily. He wanted her, and he would pursue her ruthlessly until she gave in. Admitting her feelings for him, she knew that he would not have to try too hard. He only had to look at her, and she felt weak enough to give him anything he wanted. She had to get away, because she could not stand it much longer.

Amy rose early the next morning and finished the typing that she had started the day before. When it was finished, and she had rinsed the breakfast dishes, she put the work in a folder and made a list of the shopping she would need for the evening meal.

Dressed in a bright floral skirt that swung elegantly around her long slim legs, and a white short-sleeved blouse, she felt cool and poised as she walked down to the village.

She had to pass Old Farm Cottage on the way, and she could not help glancing up at the path. It was a low, whitewashed building, and it looked as deserted as ever. A low black sports car was parked outside the front door. Fast and powerful like its owner, she thought ruefully. As she walked past, deep in thought, the front door opened and Matt walked out. Seeing him, she put her head down and walked on, hoping that he had not noticed her. He had. She heard him calling her name, and ignored him. Then he was beside her, and she could see from the mocking amusement on his face that her pretence had not worked.

He looked incredibly attractive even in the paint-stained black trousers that moulded his lean hips and strong legs, and the sleeveless black vest, also liberally smeared with paint, that left his powerful arms and shoulders bare.

'How are you today, apart from a little hard of hearing?' His voice was amused, unlike his eyes, which were narrowed in piercing scrutiny on her face.

Amy flushed, feeling ungrateful. He had saved her life, after all. 'I'm fine, thank you—no ill-effects at all. I do appreciate what you did,' she stumbled over her thanks, unnerved and distracted by his all-seeing stare.

'I'm surprised,' he drawled slowly, his eyes cooling under the heavy lids. 'I'd have thought death before dishonour fitted you perfectly.' He had noticed how stiff and grudging she was, and he was irritated.

'Matt, please——' she implored him, not wanting another argument.

His eyes flickered contemptuously. 'Please what, Amy?' he taunted. 'Do you think I don't know what goes on in that beautiful head of yours? Don't forget, I know you . . .' he paused, his eyes filled with sardonic amusement, 'intimately'. This final word was spoken softly, mockingly, and Amy was incensed. How could she forget?

'I don't know what you mean, but I do know that you're no gentleman,' she retorted heatedly.

Matt laughed out loud at that. 'And what's your definition of a gentleman, my love? Someone who never mentions sex?' He was deliberately misunderstanding her, and she wanted to smack the mocking smile from his face.

'You know what I mean,' she muttered stiffly, barely controlling her temper.

'And you know what I mean,' he responded smoothly. 'Has there been anyone else for you, Amy?' His voice had changed. It was careful and controlled.

'Yes,' she snapped angrily. 'I've had dozens of lovers since you.' It was a lie, of course, she had let nobody near her after Matt. She had not even been properly kissed. Loving him as she did, she had never considered another man, but she was not going to let him know that.

Matt's eyes darkened ominously at her words, his fists clenching at his sides, tensing the bulging muscles of his arms.

'Dozens?' His voice was deceptively quiet.

'Yes, and most of them better than you,' she cried recklessly.

His arms shot out to grab her, holding her still as he moved his mouth down to hers. His kiss was savage and angry, his lips cruel as they parted hers, but she did not care. She wondered if she had deliberately taunted him to this end. Her slim arms slid round his neck of their own accord, her fingers stroking his thick black hair feverishly. His instant response was to hold her closer, straining her responsive body against the hard wall of his chest, his lips gentle on hers.

'Dear God, I want you,' he muttered, his voice low and thick with desire. 'Come back to the house.'

'No,' her voice was strong and clear, as she forced herself out of the ecstasy of his embrace. 'Never again, Matt.'

'I don't believe you, you will in the end,' he replied, still breathing heavily, his hand cupping her chin, conviction in his eyes.

She shook her head, but he smiled knowingly, refusing to believe her. Amy knocked his hand from her throat.

'No!' she emphasised firmly again, and walked away from him, not looking back. He did not follow her, and she was surprised, and a little disappointed.

Usually he always had the last word. She thought about what he had said. Was she so transparent? He was so very sure that she would come back to him, and whatever she said failed to convince him otherwise. His confidence still irritated her. It was a pity that they could not have a civilised conversation, but every time they met, sparks flew between them.

Reaching the village, Amy delivered the letters and did the shopping, chatting to people she knew absently, Matt dominating her thoughts.

After lunch, having packed her grandfather off to Seth Greenwood's, she cleaned the cottage thoroughly. By the time she had finished, some hours later, everything was shining. She set the table with gleaming cutlery and sparkling glasses, pleased with the effect, as she stood back to admire it. Unwilling to admit it, even to herself, she felt a faint flicker of excitement at the thought of Matt coming to dinner. Three years without him had been lonely, and she had to admit that after the initial shock she was pleased to see him again. She had nothing to be ashamed of, her love for him had been pure and trusting, and the physical side of their relationship had merely been the fulfilment of that love.

It was Matt who had traded in deceit. Even now he was still acting like a free man. It was strange, because she had known him to be an honest, straightforward person. She frowned, confused, sure that she would never understand him. Sighing, she went upstairs to shower. Her hard work during the afternoon had left her hot and sticky, and she stepped under the cooling jet of water with relief. Winding a towel round herself when she got out, she walked into her bedroom and opened the wardrobe, scanning its contents for something to suitable to wear. She chose an apricot silk dress in a slim-fitting elegant style. She knew that she looked good in it, the pale colour complemented her smooth, tanned skin and golden eyes. Drying her hair, she coiled it into a Grecian knot on the top of her head. The effect was stunning, leaving bare the delicate thrust of her chin and the long grace of her vulnerable neck, and Amy was well pleased. She applied make-up sparingly, stroking gold shadow lightly over her eyelids and mascara on to her thick lashes, the final touch being a colourless lip gloss. On her ears she hung huge hoops of gold, pleased with the exotic look they gave her, then she dressed and slipped her feet into matching apricot sandals.

Studying herself in the full-length mirror, she was satisfied with the glossy, elegant woman that stared back at her. She was perfect—a perfect match for Matt Cavanagh. Running lightly downstairs, she slipped an apron carefully over her head, pausing to greet her grandfather as he came in, and set about preparing the meal. When everything was ready she sat down with a cigarette. It was seven-fifteen, and she inhaled deeply, trying to calm the nerves that fluttered in her stomach.

Sam Lawrence came downstairs in his best suit, and Amy hugged him. 'You look very smart,' she smiled.

'And you look beautiful,' he replied honestly, pleased at her compliment.

A loud knock on the door interrupted them, and Sam went to answer it, while Amy sank back into her chair, suddenly trembling.

Matt filled the room, dark and incredibly attractive in a blue suit.

'Hello, Amy.' His voice was warm and polite, and his eyes narrowed darkly as they slid over her. 'You look very lovely.' His husky compliment made her heart beat faster. He handed a bottle to her grandfather. 'I've brought some wine.'

Realising that she had not spoken, Amy smiled at Matt slowly. 'Hello, Matt,' she said softly.

'Would you like a drink before dinner, Mr Cavanagh?' Her grandfather was on his best behaviour, Amy thought, touched.

'Please. And it's Matt.'

'Right, Matt. Whisky?'

'Straight, please.' Matt was being gentle and polite, and Amy could not keep her eyes off him.

'What would you like, Amy?' her grandfather asked, breaking into her thoughts.

'A small sherry please, Granddad.' She got to her feet, as he handed her a glass. 'I'll just check on the meal,' she murmured, and made her escape to the kitchen, leaving Matt and her grandfather chatting about Cornwall.

She stirred a few pans absently, and swigged back her sherry quickly, hoping that it would make her feel calmer. She was just drinking the last of it when Matt entered the kitchen.

'Hitting the bottle, my love?' he taunted softly.

'Do you want something?' she asked sweetly, glancing hungrily at his broad shoulders.

'Your grandfather's looking for a corkscrew, and I just wondered if you needed any help.' He was staring at her, flame in his eyes.

'What help can you give? You can't cook, can you?' she replied sarcastically. His expression was blank, so she elaborated, 'You told Granddad that you couldn't cook. You wormed your way in here under false pretences. I think you're despicable!' He was too near, too attractive, and she had to hit back, to fight the desire inside her.

Matt flashed her a grim little smile, his dark eyes flashing warning. 'Be careful, Amy, don't try me too far.' His voice was low and threatening, and turning on his heel, he left the kitchen.

Amy sighed heavily. She was tired of all the antagonism between them. She had started it this time, and she regretted it, but she had no defence against him except words. Whenever he came near her, every fibre of her being responded to him, and harsh words were her only shield against his attraction.

Satisfied that everything was under control, she piled three avocado dishes on to a tray, and taking a deep breath, walked into the lounge.

The meal was an unqualified success. The steak was tender and juicy, the vegetables perfectly cooked, and the salad crisp and refreshing, and both men ate heartily. Her grandfather and Matt did most of the talking, and Amy sat silently, drinking a lot of wine, and trying to relax. A light strawberry flan with fresh cream was followed by cheese and coffee, and enjoyed by everyone.

Throughout the meal Amy felt Matt's eyes upon her, a curious brooding expression on his face. She was careful not to look at him. The wine had made her feel a little dizzy, and her eyes were brilliant gold in her flushed face. As they sat back replete, Matt offered her a cigarette. Taking one from him, she leaned towards him for a light, and misery engulfed her as she remembered how he had lit her cigarettes for her, once, placing them between her lips with his gentle smile. Suddenly the evening was flat, and she wanted to get away. Her feelings were confused, and she felt absurd for dressing so carefully. What had she hoped to achieve? There was nothing between her and Matt any more, and however good she looked, that could not be changed. She stubbed out her cigarette viciously, suddenly tired. Her grandfather was showing Matt the wood carvings that he spent his spare time on and Matt was admiring them, with honesty. Watching them talk, their heads bent over the small objects, Amy could see the gentle, caring side of Matt, that he had not shown her since he had come here. Her eyes filled with tears, and she left the room quietly and unnoticed, filled with self-pity.

She washed the dishes slowly, a dull ache throbbing in her temples. Probably all the wine that she had drunk, she thought ruefully. Matt came into the kitchen as she was drying the last plate.

'Amy, I wanted to help,' he said, still staring intently at her.

'Too late, they're all finished,' she answered with a brightness she did not feel. 'Would you excuse me if I went to bed?'

'Are you ill?' He turned her towards him with gentle hands, scanning her face with concern.

'No. I've just got a throbbing headache.' That at least was true, she thought dully, her eyes on the pulse that beat steadily in his strong brown throat.

'You drank too much wine,' he answered quietly, his fingers moving soothingly on her shoulders, softly exploring the fine bones.

'That's nothing to do with you,' she retorted, with a flash of her former spirit.

'Perhaps not,' he conceded drily. 'Go and lie down, and I'll tell your grandfather. He's a good man, Amy, I like him.'

'I know, he's a wonderful man. At least we agree on that,' she said softly, provocatively, suddenly aware of the spell that was winding around them, binding them together in the small dark room. Matt smiled down at her, a warm expression in his eyes that she had not seen for three long years. He bent his head slowly and kissed the corner of her mouth with soft lips.

'Go and lie down, Amy,' he repeated. 'I can see the pain in your eyes.'

She turned away slowly, breaking the spell unwillingly, and went upstairs.

Her headache was worse, as she slid out of her dress, leaving it where it fell, and lay down. The room was mercifully black and cool, and she could hear the two men talking downstairs. She could hear Matt's deep, amused laugh. She was happy that they got on so well together. During the last couple of days her antagonism towards Matt had faded. She still loved him with all the passion she had felt at eighteen, and it did not even matter that he had nearly broken her heart. He was back in her life, and she was glad. Her self-defensive anger was ridiculous. She wondered how his wife could bear to spend so much time away from him, as she drifted into a light, troubled sleep that deepened into restful slumber with the disappearance of her bad dreams.

She slept late next morning, wakened by her grandfather holding a cup of coffee. She struggled into alertness slowly.

'Granddad, you shouldn't,' she groaned, and then smiled. 'But I'm glad you did.' She sipped the hot coffee gratefully.

'Is your headache better?' he asked.

'Yes, it's gone. I'm sorry about last night,' she said, remembering her abrupt departure.

'It doesn't matter. He's a good man, Amy.' Her grandfather was serious as he spoke.

'That's what he said about you,' she laughed, not really wanting to discuss Matt Cavanagh's good points so early in the morning. 'And he's married,' she finished firmly.

Sam Lawrence shook his head. They would have to work it out between them. 'Do you still love him, Amy?' he asked.

Amy's face sobered at the unexpected question. 'Yes, I still love him,' she whispered sadly. 'You'd think after three years it would be finished, but I don't think I'll ever stop loving him.'

'It'll work itself out, you'll see.' Her grandfather was trying to comfort her, and she appreciated it.

Managing a weak smile, she replied without conviction, 'I hope you're right.' She finished her coffee. 'That was lovely, but I must get up. Have you had breakfast?'

'Yes, and I've made some for you, by way of saying thanks for that wonderful meal last night. I know it was difficult, but you faced up to him, and I'm proud of you, lass.' His face was kind and smiling and Amy was glad that she had gone through with it.

'I love you, Granddad,' she whispered huskily.

Sam Lawrence hugged her tightly, his eyes misty. 'Aye, well, come and get your breakfast.'

Suddenly hungry, Amy jumped out of bed, ready now to face the new day.

She dressed carefully for her dinner date with Howard that evening. The blue suit that she chose was cool and sophisticated, and with her hair in a neat chignon she knew that Howard would be pleased with her smart, poised appearance. She was ready at half past seven, with enough time to set out her grandfather's dinner. He looked up smiling as she put his meal on to the table.

'Amy, you look lovely. Are you going out with Matt?'

'No, I'm not!' she replied shortly, wishing that she was. 'Howard is taking me out to dinner.' Why did it sound so flat and uninteresting even to her own ears?

Her grandfather frowned slightly, but only said, 'Well, have a good evening, love.'

The knock on the door heralded Howard's arrival, and kissing her grandfather and grabbing her handbag, Amy left the cottage without further explanation.

They drove to a quiet restaurant well known to them both, some seven miles away. Obviously pleased to see her, Howard was easy company, and Amy began to relax.

A rich farmer, whose first love was the string of racehorses that he owned, he had met her by chance a little over a year after she had come to Cornwall. On her grandfather's suggestion she had gone to his stables one day, to enquire about riding facilities. It had been fairly obvious at this first meeting that Howard found her attractive, but Amy had been totally uninterested and had frozen his gentle advances, her heart still too raw to even consider a new relationship with a man. He had pursued her with gentle persistence however, at casual meetings usually engineered by him, until finally Amy had agreed to have dinner with him. He was light, amusing company on that first date, but she had made it clear that she wanted nothing more than uncomplicated friendship, and Howard had been forced to accept this.

Gradually their friendship became warmer, but Amy's reserve never disappeared, and she never confided in Howard about Matt. Despite Howard's desire for a deeper relationship, she could not give him any more of herself than she did already.

Watching him now as they ate, she wondered why she could not love him, or feel anything other than fondness for him. At thirty-five he was, she thought detachedly, very attractive. He was tall and strongly built, with fair good looks and an attractive personality, but he never made her heart beat faster, as Matt could, merely by looking at her.

Bringing her attention back to the food with a small sigh, she smiled at Howard and asked him about one of his horses that had broken its leg some months before. He loved talking about his horses, and Amy enjoyed his enthusiasm and the animation in his face as he chatted.

The meal was pleasant and, comfortably replete, they were leaving the restaurant, when Matt stood before them blocking their exit. The smile died on Amy's lips as she encountered the hard anger in his dark, hooded eyes. His glance slid to Howard's possessive arm around Amy's waist, and his mouth thinned ominously. However, when he spoke his voice gave no indication of his fury.

'Amy. How are you today?'

So casual, so urbane, she thought angrily, knowing that Howard's curious eyes were upon her.

'I'm much better, thank you,' she replied tightly. 'Let me introduce you, Howard. Matt Cavanagh—Howard Jordan.'

The two men nodded curtly, sizing each other up, Howard wary, Matt cold and confident. Too damned confident, thought Amy furiously, retaliating by sliding her arm around Howard's waist, and knowing the pleasure of inciting the violence in Matt's eyes.

'You'll join me for a drink?' Casually spoken, Amy knew that it was a command. But she had Howard to protect her, and even though her heart was hammering wildly, she defied him.

'No, thank you, Matt, we're just leaving,' she said sweetly.

'Another time, perhaps.' Always polite, Howard was trying to make up for Amy's rudeness.

'Of course.' Matt dismissed them gracefully, but glancing into his eyes, Amy knew she would pay for this another time.

Shivering uncontrollably, and regretting her actions, she left the restaurant, her arm still around Howard's waist.

'Matt Cavanagh ... that name seems familiar.' Howard turned towards her as they drove home.

'He's a sculptor—quite famous, actually,' Amy replied carefully.

'Of course, I remember now. Have you known him long?' Howard's question was mildly spoken, but Amy knew that she would have to give him an answer.

'He exhibited at the gallery where I worked in London, and he's renting Old Farm Cottage for a while,' she said, wishing she could control the tremor in her voice.

'Quite a coincidence.' Howard was thoughtful, sensing that Amy was holding something back.

'I suppose so.' Amy wanted this conversation at an end so desperately that her change of subject was clumsy. 'Will you be playing cricket tomorrow?' she asked. So false, so bright, but it seemed to work, and the journey home was completed without further embarrassment for Amy.

Thanking Howard for a lovely evening, she allowed him to kiss her forehead briefly before sliding out of the car.

This situation with Matt Cavanagh was getting out of hand, she thought wearily, as she made her way upstairs to bed. She could not, would not let him affect her friendship with Howard. He was something strong and secure in her life, a life that

Matt had turned upside down again, and she needed something to cling to.

Her punishment for refusing Matt in the restaurant came the next day. Walking across the fields to the village to avoid walking past Matt's gate, she came face to face with him. He had been lying in the summer grass, but got slowly and gracefully to his feet as she approached.

They faced each other as enemies, Amy desperate for escape, cursing her bad luck, and filled with longing and the ache of love. Her hungry glance took in the fact that his chest was bare, he had obviously been sunbathing, and the sight of his powerful brown body sent her head spinning round as she sought her escape.

Matt smiled slightly, his eyes veiled. 'You won't get away, Amy,' he said softly, reading her mind. 'Not until I've talked to you.'

'About what?' At last she looked him straight in the face.

'Is Jordan your lover?' he asked harshly.

'That's none of your business!' she snapped angrily. He took a step towards her, blocking out the sunshine, and fear made her retaliate dishonestly, 'Yes, he's my lover.'

She heard his swift intake of breath as his arms shot out and grabbed her.

'Let me go,' she whispered, trying to prise his strong fingers from her shoulder.

Matt ignored her, and almost despite themselves his fingers slid beneath her thin silk blouse to caress the soft skin and fine bones beneath.

'Tell me again,' he commanded, his voice dangerously soft.

'Howard is my lover,' she repeated clearly, willing to say anything to make him let her go.

'You little bitch!' he grated, as he lowered his head.

Amy desperately tried to evade his mouth, but his hand slid up from her shoulder to grasp her chin, holding her still as his lips found hers. As their mouths touched, Amy's arms came around Matt's neck of their own volition, and she swayed against him. He took her weight and lowered them both back down into the sweet-smelling grass. His kiss was deep and passionate and so sweetly demanding that Amy could not deny him as her lips parted beneath his. Her hands were caressing the warm, hair-coarsened skin of his chest, and somehow her blouse was undone and his lips were gentle at her breasts. She opened her eyes then and looked down at him, at his proud, dark head bent in reverence to her body, and knew that if she did not get away immediately she would be lost. He lifted his head then, sensing her gaze.

'Is Jordan your lover?' he repeated, his eyes glittering strangely and demanding truth.

'No,' she admitted finally. She could not lie any longer.

Matt sighed heavily. 'Amy——' His dark gaze slid over her beautiful body. 'God, I'm so hungry for you,' he groaned achingly, pressing his lips to the hollow between her breasts.

Amy closed her eyes, fighting the ecstasy he offered. 'Matt . . .?'

He lifted his head and she took the opportunity to move a little away from him. She had to get away.

He was still looking at her questioningly, hunger burning in his eyes. She fumbled with the buttons of her blouse.

'Please let me go. I've told you what you wanted to know.' Her voice was cool and strong, and she met his eyes steadily.

Matt rolled on to his back immediately, his mouth tightening. 'Go,' he said harshly.

She stared at him for a moment, unable to believe that he was making it so easy for her, then she scrambled to her feet and walked away, not looking back until she reached the gate of the field. When she did look back, he was still lying in the same place, still and alone, gazing up into the sky. She was suddenly very miserable.

She did not see Matt for a couple of days, and although she told herself that she was glad, she missed him. She had grown used to seeing him practically every day.

One sunny morning nearly a week later she was hanging out the weekly wash in the garden when he walked up behind her. She turned quickly, seeing his shadow falling across the grass.

'Good morning, Amy,' he greeted her politely, looking lean and fit in his usual tight denim jeans, and a green checked shirt.

'Hello, Matt.' Amy suddenly felt nervous and absurdly shy. She carried on pegging out the clothes, supremely aware that his dark, unfathomable eyes were watching intently every movement of her long, graceful body. Dressed in brief white shorts and a sleeveless white tee-shirt, she felt practically naked under that smouldering gaze.

'Why do you stare at me?' she asked, flushing, but not turning to look at him.

'Does it embarrass you?' he asked, amused.

'A little,' she admitted.

'I stare at you because you're beautiful, because you have a fluid grace of movement that fascinates me. Come, Amy, you know why I stare at you.'

She could not tell whether he was laughing at her

or not. Biting back the sarcastic retort that sprang to her lips, remembering her promise to herself, not to start any antagonism between them, she turned to face him.

'I'm just about to make some coffee. Would you like some?' She allowed herself the luxury of gazing into his face as she asked.

He looked tired, lines of strain apparent around his mouth, and suddenly she felt worried about him. Impatiently she pushed this thought out of her mind as ridiculous. Matt Cavanagh did not need anybody to worry about him.

'Yes, coffee will be fine,' he answered quietly, and followed her into the cottage. He sat at the table while she put the kettle on, strangely silent, watching her deft movements absently. The quiet stretched between them, until Amy had to break it.

'Do you . . . er . . . that is . . . er . . . did you come for anything in particular?' she stammered, passing her tongue nervously over her dry lips.

He sipped his coffee slowly before replying, a faint smile playing around the grim line of his mouth.

'I've heard that you do secretarial work. I've got some letters that need typing.'

'Yes, I do.' Slightly piqued that his reason for coming was business, she was nonetheless glad to have something to talk about. 'Have you brought them with you?'

'No. Do you work from here?' His voice was expressionless, his eyes remote as they scanned her face.

'Yes, if you'd like to drop them in, I could do them for you this afternoon.' What was the matter with him, he seemed miles away.

'What I really want is somebody at the cottage. Somebody to answer the phone when I'm working.'

His dark eyes were cool, his mouth mocking the confusion in her face.

Amy felt irritated, sure that this was a trick. She could not spend long hours at his cottage every day, alone with him. Added to which his taunting threat on the beach, his confidence that she would become his lover again, made the idea impossible.

She glared at him. 'Then I suggest you hire a full-time secretary.' Ice dripped from her voice, belied by the heated anger in her gold eyes.

Matt's mocking smile deepened. He leaned over, and ran his finger slowly down her cheek. 'What's the matter, Amy, can't you trust yourself?' His low, amused tone outraged her. He was too close to the truth.

'It's you that I don't trust, Matt Cavanagh. I can see right through you and your disgusting little schemes!' she choked, hitting his hand away from her face.

Still laughing, Matt rose indolently to his feet. 'Thanks for the coffee. You ought to have red hair with that temper,' he said mildly. He ducked out of the door, barely missing the cup that she flung after him. She heard his deep, amused laughter as he walked down the path, and cursed him.

CHAPTER EIGHT

AMY went for a walk after lunch, a long, exhausting walk. She felt full of pent-up energy, and strangely restless. She realised now, since Matt had come into her life again, that over the past couple of years she had been living to half her full potential. She was a young and healthy woman living the life of a middle-aged matron.

All of a sudden she wanted to travel, dance until dawn, and have a family. The break-up of her affair with Matt had dulled her senses, letting her choose the easy way out—secure, lonely days, with no purpose but survival.

She strode along the cliffs, walking miles, and not feeling tired. The sea air filled her head with the potency of wine and she felt exhilarated.

Suddenly she was standing on the edge of a new life and she was going to jump. Perhaps she would leave Cornwall. Matt: her thoughts returned to him. They had no future together. He did not love her. Life without him would be difficult—no one would ever replace him in her heart—but she had done it before, and she could do it again.

She had not seen Howard since the incident in the restaurant. He had telephoned twice and asked her out on both occasions, but she had put him off. He deserved the truth, of course, but in her weakness and inability to cope with Matt she had used him as an anchor. It was unfair, and in her present positive mood she realised that their friendship would have to end.

It was sad, but he felt so much more than she that they could never remain friends. Perhaps she would telephone.

The rain started without her noticing. She looked up just in time to see the heavens opening, and was soaked to the skin within minutes. She was miles from home.

'Damn!' She swore angrily out loud. It would take her at least half an hour to get back. Turning, she began to run. Forty minutes later she was only a few hundred yards from the cottage and covered with mud. The exertion of running all the way had left her hot and sweating, even as she was shivering with cold.

The storm had darkened the sky ominously, and noticing that the cottage was in darkness she assumed that her grandfather was out, taking shelter somewhere. She hurried into the cottage, thankful to be home. The windows were open and rain was leaking heavily into the lounge. Amy groaned as she remembered the washing, still hanging out in the garden. Although there was not much point, she might as well bring it in. Turning towards the kitchen door, she saw her grandfather, and her stomach turned over sickeningly.

'Oh, God, Granddad!' Her shriek was hysterical, as she ran over to him. He was lying inert at the bottom of the stairs, one leg twisted unnaturally beneath his body. He was unconscious, or maybe he was dead. Panic rose in her, and she could not touch him. Trembling uncontrollably, tears pouring down her face, her one thought was that she should not move him. She had to get help. Picking up the phone, she found it was dead. The storm must have brought down the lines. Matt—he would know what to do. Uncaring of the thunder and lightning, she ran wildly from the house, trembling so much that her legs could hardly carry her. Please, please, she prayed silently as she stumbled through the rain, let him be there. Let him know what to do.

She ran up the path and banged on his door. Out of breath, she felt her heart was bursting, it was beating so fast. There was no answer. She banged again, louder, leaning weakly against the door. He's got to be in, she chanted to herself desperately.

Finally, after what seemed like an age, the door opened, and Matt stood there, frowning. 'What the . . .' he began.

'Matt . . .!' Amy gasped with relief and collapsed into his arms, unable to stand up a moment longer.

He picked her up and took her inside, his eyes darkening angrily, his mouth compressed thinly as he looked over her. She was covered with mud and soaked to the skin, and shivering sobs were racking her body and tears poured down her face, as she fought for breath.

'Amy, what in God's name is the matter?'

'Matt—it's Granddad. He's just lying there—he might be dead—the telephone won't work, and I don't know what to do—help me . . .' Her voice trailed off weakly, reaction setting in and making her sway towards him. Matt poured some brandy into a glass, and thrust it into her shaking hands. 'Drink this now.' he ordered.

She gulped it down, coughing as it burned her throat, and filled her body with warmth.

'Is he at the cottage?' Matt's voice was quiet and authoritative.

'Yes, we must go now.'

Ignoring her, he picked up the phone. It was dead. He took her by the shoulders and forced her to look up at him.

'Amy, I'll come back with you now. We'll have to take him to the hospital, if he needs it, in my car. You'll have to help me.' His voice was clear and demanding, and Amy nodded.

Putting his arm about her shoulders to steady her, he led her out to the car, and drove to the cottage. Still shivering, Amy felt so tired and weak that she could hardly move. Matt jumped out of the car as soon as they got there and strode inside. Amy followed, desperately, thankful that he had taken charge. Matt was crouched over her grandfather as she entered.

'He's unconscious,' he said grimly. 'And I think his leg's broken. We'll have to take him to the hospital.'

'Is . . . is he . . . going to die?' Her voice was barely a whisper, as she stared at him.

'No, but we need to move fast. Get some pillows and a blanket, and a coat for yourself, then go and open the back of the car.' His orders were curt and concise, and Amy responded automatically, her hysteria disappearing under his calm control.

She rushed upstairs, grabbing pillows and blankets from her bed, and ran down with them. Matt had lifted her grandfather into his arms, and was waiting. She opened the back of the car, the rain soaking her anew, and Matt placed her grandfather gently on the back seat, covering him with the blankets.

He turned to Amy. 'You'll have to direct me to the hospital.'

'Of course,' she nodded as she slid into the car. She kept glancing over her shoulder at her grandfather. His face was so white and he looked so old. Fresh tears ran down her face. He mustn't die, she thought despairingly.

Matt read her thoughts. 'He won't die, Amy,' he

said gently, reassuringly.

'I'm so frightened for him,' she whispered tearfully.

'He'll be all right,' Matt repeated. 'Now, I need some directions.' Amy directed him, responding automatically to the command in his voice. He kept his eyes on the road, and glancing at his long lean hands, competent on the steering-wheel, she trusted him.

The rain was still torrential, making the road almost impassable, but after what seemed like hours they were driving through the hospital gates. Matt drove straight to the casualty entrance, the car skidding to a standstill as he jumped out.

'Stay here,' he ordered, and disappeared through the swing doors. Seconds later he reappeared with two white-coated men, carrying a stretcher. They carried the old man into the hospital, Matt helped Amy out of the car, and they followed. Sam Lawrence was seen immediately by a brisk young doctor, and Amy sat outside the curtained cubicle, numb and distressed, while he was examined. Matt talked to the doctor for about five minutes, and although she tried, Amy could not catch what they were saying. She looked into Matt's face, dread in her dull gold eyes, when he returned to her side.

'He's going to be all right, Amy,' he said truthfully. 'I'm taking you home now.'

'No, I'm staying here until I can see him.' Unconvinced, she did not want to leave, but Matt took her arm urgently.

'You won't be able to see him for hours. They have to set his leg, and treat his other injuries.' Although his voice was slow and patient, his dark eyes warned her to do as she was told. 'You're coming home with me, and I'll bring you back later,' he said firmly, pulling her to her feet.

She was still shivering violently with cold and shock, and Matt shook his head.

'You're going to get pneumonia if you don't get these wet clothes off soon!' He was not going to argue, so she allowed him to guide her out of the hospital.

As they drove on to the main road, she glanced at his stern profile. 'Is he really going to be all right?' she asked, needing reassurance.

Matt answered honestly. 'He's seriously ill. At his age, a broken limb is always dangerous, but he's tough, and the doctor told me that he should pull through. That's the truth.'

Listening to his quiet words, Amy felt tears welling up in her eyes again. Dismayed, she pressed her knuckles into her mouth, but she could not stop. Sobs racked her body again and, swearing, Matt stopped the car.

'I'm sorry,' she hiccoughed weakly.

'Amy, Amy, don't cry, my love,' he groaned, pulling her into his arms, his face dark with concern as he comforted her.

She leaned against the broad hardness of his chest as he soothed her. His arms were so warm and secure that she did not want to leave them. Finally, though, she pulled away, wiping her tears with cold fingers. 'You always seem to be comforting me,' she remarked with an attempt at lightness.

He smiled. 'Whenever you need me.' Turning on the engine he said, 'Are you okay?'

'Yes, but I can't seem to stop shivering,' she answered.

Driving fast, Matt reached his cottage within ten minutes.

'Come on,' he said, as he got out.

Amy did not move. 'I want to go home,' she muttered stubbornly.

'Amy——' his voice was exasperated, as he stared at her, 'I don't intend to seduce you. Have you got a fire going at home? Have you got hot water?' She shook her head wordlessly, knowing that she had made a fool of herself, and again Matt sighed irritably. 'Well, I have, and they're at your disposal. No strings attached.' His sarcasm cut into her, and she stumbled out of the car feeling stupid.

Once inside, he led her straight up to the bathroom and began running a hot bath.

'I can manage,' she said shortly.

His mouth tightened, but he remained silent. Reaching into the airing cupboard he pulled out a huge flannelette nightdress. Grinning, he passed it to her.

'It must belong to the owner's wife. You can wear it until your clothes are dry. As you can see, it's quite respectable.'

She grabbed it, shooting him a withering look, and his mouth twitched as he turned to leave the room.

'Pass me your clothes as you undress.' Noticing her frown, he explained dryly, 'The sooner they're dry, the sooner we can return to the hospital. What a suspicious little mind you've got, Amy!'

Slamming the door behind him, she stripped off her wet clothes thankfully and wrapped herself in a towel. She opened the door a crack, hot colour staining her cheeks, and thrust the soggy articles into his hands, ignoring his mocking grin as he took them. Stepping into the steaming bath was sheer delight. Her shivering gradually stopped, as the heat flooded her weary bones. She lay soaking for long minutes, feeling her tense muscles relaxing, and the aching in her limbs easing away. Then she scrubbed herself clean and shampooed her hair, rejoicing in the feeling of cleanliness after being covered with mud. She stepped out of the bath reluctantly, pink and glowing, into thick fluffy towels, and drying herself quickly, slipped into the capacious nightdress. It fell to the floor, many sizes too big for her, but as Matt had so sarcastically said, it was respectable.

Behind all her actions was worry about her grandfather. She trusted Matt, she realised, even though she had denied it. If he said her grandfather would pull through, she believed him.

She combed out her hair, leaving it loose to dry quicker, and went downstairs.

Matt had changed, and was pouring out tea as she went into the room. Her clothes were drying on a clothes horse in front of the fire. He spoke without turning, sensing her presence. 'Sit by the fire and drink this tea.'

Meekly Amy curled up on the comfortable leather armchair, curving her legs beneath her and enjoying the warmth.

Matt's eyes were darkly enigmatic as he passed her the mug of tea. She looked young, vulnerable and breathtakingly lovely to him. He sighed. 'You look like a little girl in that nightdress,' he said smiling gently.

'It's enormous,' she laughed in reply. Then, seriously, 'I can't thank you enough, Matt, for all you've done. You were the first person I thought of when ... when I found Granddad. I knew that you'd know what to do——' She stopped suddenly, embarrassed by her admission.

Matt was still smiling at her, pleased that her trust in him was returning. 'I'm glad you thought of me. If ever you need any help, you know where I am,' he answered slowly, his eyes dark and intent on her face.

Amy looked away, sipping her scalding tea gratefully, a warm glow inside her at his sincerely spoken words.

'As soon as your clothes are dry, we'll drive back to the hospital. Do you feel strong enough?'

'Yes, I'm fine now,' she answered eagerly, wanting to get back as soon as possible. She frowned. 'Do you think they'll let us see him?'

Matt took both her hands in his. 'I don't know, Amy, but if they do don't be upset if he looks bad. He's had a nasty accident, and he'll be feeling pretty rotten. Do you understand? Don't expect too much.' His words were strong and soothing and, nodding, Amy felt immeasurably glad that he was with her. He dropped her hands and stood up, stretching wearily, flexing the powerful muscles of his shoulders. He handed her the dry clothes and she went upstairs to dress. Her hair had dried by the fire, and she felt much better. She spent some minutes inwardly composing herself for what she knew would be an ordeal, then went downstairs to join Matt.

'Are you ready?' His eyes flickered over her darkly.

'Yes, and thanks again for all you've done.'

Impulsively she leaned up and kissed his hard cheek. She felt him stiffen, and immediately regretted her action. Cursing herself, she walked out to the car.

The rain had stopped, and the air smelled sweet and cool, although the sky was still ominously grey as evening approached. Matt manoeuvred the sleek car on to the main road, and Amy glanced at him from beneath her eyelashes. His strong profile was remote and hard as he lit a cigarette and offered her one, without taking his eyes off the road. She took it thankfully, hoping it would soothe her ravaged nerves.

They drove to the hospital in silence, Matt seeming preoccupied, deep in thought, and Amy feeling worried and miserable.

Matt helped her out of the car as soon as they arrived, and with his hand at her elbow guided her into the hospital. He found out from the enquiry desk where her grandfather was, and Amy noticed the nurse behind the desk openly eyeing him with interest, his devastating smile leaving her openmouthed and flushed, as she practically fell over herself to help him. Amy turned away, jealousy clawing at her cruelly. She knew that Matt was immensely attractive to women, she had seen them watching him, flirting with him, they were drawn to him like a magnet. And every time she saw it, jealousy reared its ugly head and she suffered. It was ridiculous, because she had no claim on him anyway.

Matt came back from the enquiry desk with the information, a slight smile curving his hard mouth, and Amy turned away peevishly.

Ignoring her, he guided her up the stairs to the room where her grandfather was. Under strict instructions from the nurse to stay for only a few minutes, Amy paused at the door, frightened to go in, afraid almost to see her grandfather. Noticing her fear, Matt took her hand in his, and led her inside.

Her grandfather was asleep, and as Amy stared at his tired, pale face, tears welled up in her eyes. Various bottles with drips were hanging by the bed, the tubes of which snaked up her grandfather's nose. His leg was plastered, and he looked old and very weak. She stared at him, sure he was going to die, and the tears she had tried to blink back fell down her cheeks unheeded. The room was full of machines, dominating the small frail figure that lay perfectly still in their midst. She turned away, unable to look at him any longer. At that moment the nurse popped her head round the door and told them that they would have to leave. Matt left the room with her, and Amy could hear them talking in hushed voices outside the door. She looked back at her grandfather, wanting to wake him up and ask him if he was all right. Of course she didn't, she just stared at him, and prayed that he was.

Then Matt was in the room again, taking her shoulders, and tilting up her wet face with gentle fingers.

'Don't cry, Amy. You need to be brave,' he said softly, his eyes warm and comforting.

'I know, and I'll try to be,' she whispered, mesmerised by his nearness.

'Let's go home,' his voice was incredibly weary.

Amy reached up and touched his cheek, suddenly realising what a strain it must have been for him. She had been leaning on him, relying on him all day, knowing that he could take it and disregarding his feelings. He slipped his arm around her shoulder, and they left the room. Matt drove back speedily to her cottage. Amy was thinking about her grandfather and looked up in surprise as the car slid to a halt. She got out quickly, and it was then she noticed that the front door was open. Fear shafted through her, and she turned to Matt. He was sliding out of the car, having seen the open door.

'I'll come in with you, and we'll check the house,' he said firmly, taking her hand.

The house was in darkness, unnaturally quiet, it seemed to Amy, as they walked up the path. She could hear her own heart beating, it was so quiet. Matt went in first, switching on the lights, as he did so, keeping her behind him, automatically shielding her with his body. They inspected every room, switching on lights as they went. The house was empty, untouched, and she let out a long sigh of relief.

'Will you be all right on your own?' the question was serious, but his eyes held a mocking glint as he spoke.

'Yes, I will,' she retorted, flushing at the double meaning in his words.

'Right—goodnight, Amy,' he turned on his heel and strode towards the door.

Suddenly Amy was frightened of being left alone in the empty house. 'Matt!' she called him back as he left. 'Would you stay for a while? I'm frightened.'

He halted at the sound of her voice and walked back into the room, his eyes darkly unfathomable. He saw the fear and loneliness in her face, and striding over to her pulled her into his arms with a muttered imprecation.

She wrapped her arms around him, pressing herself to the hard length of him. Under her ear, she heard his heartbeat quicken as she began to caress his back.

'Dammit, Amy, do you know what you're doing to me?' he muttered hoarsely.

She lifted her head from his chest, and stared into his face, her soft mouth parted seductively.

'Yes,' she murmured, as his mouth came down on hers.

The pressure of his lips was hungry and insistent, as he explored the sweetness of her inviting mouth. Heat flared up inside her at his touch, and she responded fully to his demanding body, wanting him to stay, needing him, loving him. She knew that he was fiercely aroused, and the knowledge excited her. His stroking hands slid beneath the silk blouse that she was wearing, his breathing forced and painful as his fingers encountered the soft skin of her waist, moving up slowly to the smooth swellings of her taut breasts.

His lips were at her throat now, nibbling gently at the sensitive cord of her neck. Desire that could no longer be denied was flooding Amy's body like fire.

'Stay with me, Matt,' she murmured, her breathing quick and uneven. Almost immediately she felt him stiffen and his hands dropped from her body, as he put her away from him. He was breathing deeply, his eyes black with desire, as he raked his hand through his thick dark hair.

'You don't know what you're asking,' he said harshly.

'I do,' she replied softly, her eyes slumbrous and inviting, her lips parted, and swollen from his kisses.

He stared at her for a moment, then swore angrily. 'For God's sake, Amy, I need a woman in my bed tonight, not a child playing games!'

Abruptly he turned away and strode quickly out of the cottage, not looking back.

The front door slammed behind him, echoing through the quiet house, and Amy was alone, deeply hurt at his cruel rejection.

CHAPTER NINE

AMY sat up in bed, wondering what was wrong, then remembered her grandfather lying in the hospital. She rubbed her eyes wearily, feeling depressed and uneasy. The sky was filled with low, forbidding clouds, dull and grey to match her mood. She struggled out of bed, her whole body aching; she supposed it was the result of getting so wet the day before.

Inevitably, her thoughts turned to Matt. She had offered herself to him, on his terms, and he had rejected her. He had proved his point. She would have been his lover again, and the thought made her bury her face miserably in her hands.

Dressing, after a quick, reviving shower, in russet corduroy trousers and a short-sleeved jumper in a complementary shade, she ran downstairs to try the phone. It was still dead, and sighing frustratedly, she slammed it down. She would have to go down to the village to see if she could phone the hospital from there. She grabbed a quick cup of coffee, unable to eat anything, then shrugging into an anorak jacket, she collected her handbag and left the cottage. She passed Matt's cottage with firmly averted eyes, and had just reached the bottom of the lane when she heard a car coming.

It was Matt's car. She walked on, keeping to the side of the road, ignoring it, but not before she had seen the two passengers. Matt was driving, the other person was a woman. The car drew up beside her, and Matt stuck his head out of the window as she walked past.

Before he had spoken, Amy had taken note of the woman beside him. Young, dark and attractive, she was eyeing Amy curiously.

'Amy . . .' she heard Matt's voice, and ignored him, walking on quickly. He shouted again, exasperation in his voice, as she quickened her pace. She heard the car door slam, and then he was beside her, grabbing her arm and spinning her round to face him.

'Amy . . . about last night . . .' he began.

Her eyes flashed anger, as she cut across him.

'Go to hell!' she spat. 'I suppose that's the *woman* you needed in your bed last night, or is it your wife?'

Matt stared at her intently for a long moment before replying, his dark eyes shuttered beneath the heavy eyelids.

'I'm not married.' His answer was quiet and distinctly spoken.

Amy, however, was in no mood to listen to him.

'Liar!' she hissed furiously, her gold eyes brilliant with rage. 'That line might work on her . . .' she tossed her proud head towards his car contemptuously, 'but I know better, and I've told you—go to hell!'

She wrenched herself from his grasp and walked stiffly away, anger and humiliation nearly blinding her. Who did he think he was trying to kid? Celine's description of Matt's wife came back to her: dark and attractive. It fitted the woman in his car perfectly, and Amy nearly choked. She would like to strangle him—slowly. It was no wonder he had rejected her; his wife would have been waiting for him at his cottage. Amy felt cheap, hurt and humiliated.

Glancing up, she realised that she had walked right past the post office without noticing it, so she had to retrace her steps. The post office phone was working, and after explaining about the accident, she rang the hospital. But they would not tell her anything. Comfortable—what did that mean? Worried, Amy arranged to go in right away.

Mrs Jenks, who ran the post office, had cut some flowers for her grandfather while Amy had been on the phone. She thrust them into Amy's hand, sending her best wishes, and Amy felt touched. It was good to know that her grandfather was well loved in the village. The other good news from Mrs Jenks was that the telephone lines would be in working order later that afternoon.

Amy bought some flowers of her own, and some fruit, then caught the bus to the hospital. Her grandfather was awake as she went into his room.

'You can only stay for about ten minutes. He'll tire very easily,' the nurse whispered.

Thanking her, Amy walked to the bed, pulling up a chair.

'How are you, Granddad?' she asked softly, taking his hand as she sat down.

'Amy—it's good to see you.' His voice was weak and tired.

'Mrs Jenks has sent you some flowers, the nurse is just getting a vase for them.'

Her grandfather nodded, his eyes closing slowly, and realising that he was asleep, Amy slipped her hand out of his. She sat watching him, worriedly, until the nurse came in with the flowers.

'He's asleep,' she whispered. 'Is he all right?'

The nurse looked at him, then turned to Amy. 'He's fine. But he's heavily sedated, I don't think he'll wake up for quite a while, so there's not much point in you staying.' Seeing Amy's worried face, she added reassuringly, 'Come back this evening, he should be feeling better then.'

Amy smiled. 'I'll do that. Thank you.'

Getting to her feet, she left the room, closing the door quietly. She would have to get in touch with Aunt Juliet, and tell her about the accident.

It was a relief to get out of the hushed, strongly-smelling atmosphere of the hospital, and she had been standing at the bus stop for about ten minutes when a black car pulled up in front of her. Matt leaned over and opened the door.

'Get in. I want to talk to you,' he ordered.

Amy's anger returned, at his overbearing tone. 'Get lost!' she snapped, turning away.

'Get in, or I'll put you in myself.' Barely controlling his temper, Matt was speaking through clenched teeth.

Sighing, Amy got into the car, turning on him angrily, as soon as the door was shut.

'What is it with you? Can't you take no for an answer? Why are you following me around?' she demanded.

'I want to talk to you,' he said coolly, but his face was dark and threatening.

Ignoring him, Amy carried on. 'Well, I don't want to talk to you,' she snapped.

'That wasn't the case yesterday when you needed my help,' he remarked grimly, his mouth tight, his dark eyes glittering dangerously.

Ashamed, Amy realised that he was right and her anger disappeared.

'I'm sorry.' Her apology was sincere and quietly spoken.

Matt turned to look at her, his cold eyes scanning her face for deceit. Finding none, he continued, 'I'm sorry, too, about last night. I was cruel—it was unforgivable.'

Flushing, Amy turned to look out of the window. 'Really, there's no need to apologise. Let's forget it,' she mumbled. She did not want to think about, let alone talk about his rejection of her.

'How's your grandfather?' Matt asked quietly.

Grateful for a change of subject Amy replied immediately, eagerly, 'He was awake for five minutes, but he still looks very weak. The nurse said he was heavily sedated, so I'm going back tonight.'

Matt watched the sad worry in her eyes as she spoke. 'I'll drive you,' he said firmly.

'No, really, I can get the bus,' she murmured, appalled at the idea of spending so much time in his company.

'Don't argue, Amy.' He sounded irritated again as he switched on the engine.

Shrugging, she sat back meekly as the car throbbed to life, and sped on to the main road. He lit a cigarette with graceful ease and offered her one, which she refused.

She glanced at him surreptitiously as he drove. He was wearing close-fitting black trousers that moulded his muscular legs, and a black shirt that emphasised his saturnine good looks. The raw magnetism that he exuded made her quiver responsively inside, just looking at him. She wanted to ask him about the woman in his car. She wanted to ask him why he had lied about being married, but she sat and gazed out of the window instead.

The car drew up outside her cottage and she immediately fumbled with the door handle.

'Thanks for the lift,' she murmured, not looking at him.

'Amy——' Matt placed a restraining hand on her arm, and she turned to find him staring at her with narrowed, unreadable eyes. He seemed to come to a decision before continuing.

'What I told you this morning was true. I'm not married.'

Amy gazed at him confused. 'But you told me . . . and Celine said . . .'

'Celine!' Matt snorted angrily. 'Celine is a very close friend of Joanne's. As far as I'm concerned, Celine is . . . easy game. I'd only have to snap my fingers . . .' His voice was openly contemptuous. He was convincing, and Amy believed him. Matt watched the confused emotions playing across her lovely open face, with dark intent eyes, before continuing.

'I've been divorced for over two years,' he said quietly, and she stared at him, speechless.

'When I met you, Amy, Joanne and I had been married for two years, but separated for over eighteen months. The marriage was a mistake, we both knew that, two weeks into it. You could say——' his mouth twisted harshly, 'that ours was a marriage of convenience. We tried to work things out, but after three months we both knew that it was hopeless. Joanne had already taken a lover when we split up.' His eyes were bleak and unseeing, as he stared at Amy.

'I'm sorry,' she said softly. 'Did you love her?' she could not resist asking.

Matt smiled, a grim little smile that did not reach his hard eyes.

'No, I never loved her, and she didn't love me. We were attracted to each other at the beginning, but as I say, it was a marriage of convenience—nothing more.'

'Convenience?' Amy stared at him curiously, unable to stop herself asking the question, needing to know the answer.

'Yes. When I came home after all those years abroad, my father was ill—he'd had two heart attacks while I'd been away, and I felt guilty about not being there—responsible, I guess.' Matt passed his hand wearily around the back of his neck.

'For some time he'd wanted to merge the business with that of an old friend—about the only friend he had left by then—Joanne's father.'

Amy sat bolt upright in her seat; she could almost guess what was coming next. Matt continued.

'Arthur, her father, wanted some security for Joanne—quite rightly, and he had the idea that if we married she would be set up for life, and I could run both companies.' He sighed heavily.

'My father, true to form, had omitted to tell Arthur that I wouldn't be going into the business, and had agreed to the whole thing.' Matt paused for a moment, and Amy kept silent, not wanting to break into his thoughts, watching the pain and anger in his face with a strange compassion.

'So the merger had been set up, the papers to be signed the day after Joanne and I married. I refused to do it, of course, and we had an almighty row the night I got back. I left the house with no intention of ever coming back, an intention I made clear to my father. His housekeeper got in touch with me about a week later—I'd told her where she could leave a message for me, if necessary, and told me that he'd had another heart attack, the night I'd left—a bad one—and they thought he might die. You can imagine how guilty I felt. I went over immediately, and as ill as he was, all he was worried about was the bloody business!' Matt's voice was bitter, and Amy knew what it was costing him to tell her all this.

'He was very disturbed and it was affecting badly any chances of recovery he had. God help me, Amy, I wanted to do something to ease him, so I agreed to the marriage. It was worth it just to see him relax. I called Joanne—we'd always got on fairly well. She was her father's daughter—business came first, and as I say, we were attracted to each other at the beginning. We were married a week later in my father's hospital room.' He shrugged defeatedly. 'It didn't matter any more, all I wanted was for my father to live—I didn't want him to die because of me. The lies, the deceits, the manipulations became unimportant. The papers were signed, and slowly my father recovered. He was never fit again, but at least he was alive. I've told you the rest—for Joanne and me, it was disastrous. She runs the business now, I believe, what she wanted all along, and she married again. Everything turned out fine,' he finished sardonically.

Amy knew by the finality of his tone that she could ask no more questions. She felt an overwhelming sense of protectiveness for him, as she put her mouth gently against his and kissed him.

'Forgive me, Matt,' she murmured against his lips, and they curved against hers as he withdrew.

'Amy, how could I not forgive you?' he said gently. Kissing her cheek, he put her away from him. 'I'll pick you up at seven, is that okay?'

She nodded, her senses still reeling, then slid out of the car and ran up the path, closing the front door as he drove off. Her legs gave way as soon as she was inside, and she sank weakly into an easy chair. She felt hurt and cold inside at the way Matt had put her from him coolly, in the car. Another rejection.

She could hardly believe that he was not married.

She knew now, with pain squeezing her heart, that his proposal to her, three years ago, had been sincere. He had intended to marry her when his divorce had come through, and she had thrown it back in his face. He did not love her now, of that she was certain, but she wondered if he ever had loved her. Groaning, she buried her head in her hands. She had run away from something that had not existed three years ago, and ruined her chance of happiness. Lighting a cigarette with trembling fingers, she tried to compose her thoughts.

When Matt had first come to Cornwall she had been angry and suspicious of his motives. She had vowed to herself that she would not become his lover again, and he had been arrogantly sure of the opposite. Yet they had slipped into an easy familiarity as the days passed. His innate gentleness and charm had softened her towards him, and of course she had never stopped loving him, even though she had tried—God, how she had tried! Her easily-ignited anger had been her only defence against the deep feelings he aroused in her, and although she had ached to hear him say that he loved her, he never had. He cared for her in the same way that he cared for everybody. And that hurt.

Now there was another woman in his life, and it was too late to find out that he had never deceived her.

She stubbed out her cigarette, despairingly, sick of thinking about the whole mess. Matt was lost to her again, and she did not think she could stand it.

The phone interrupted her thoughts, making her jump, even as she reached for it eagerly. It was only the engineer, checking the line. As soon as she replaced the receiver, she hunted through the sideboard for Aunt Juliet's number, Finding it, she dialled Germany direct, hoping that her aunt was in. She was.

'Amy, my dear!' her aunt's pleasure came clearly across the long distance. 'How are you? How's Dad?'

Amy cleared her throat. 'Actually, Aunt Juliet, that's why I'm phoning. Granddad has had an accident, and broken his leg. He's in hospital.'

'Good God, is he bad?' her aunt's voice was worried.

'No—that is, he's pretty bad at the moment, but he'll pull through. The only problem really is his age. I thought you ought to know.' Amy grimaced; she hated giving bad news over the telephone.

'Of course, dear, I'm glad you phoned. I'll try and get Harry to take some time off work so that we can fly over and see him. You'll send our love, when you see him?'

'I will, Aunt Juliet. There's nothing to worry about, you know.' She tried to sound reassuring, because she could tell that her aunt was worried.

'I know, dear, but I'd like to see him, especially if he's ill. By the way, Amy, Joni and Terry will be flying over tomorrow. Will you be able to put them up? It doesn't really matter if you can't. It was going to be a surprise, but with this news of Dad, I thought I'd better tell you. They'll be leaving little Susan here, which will be nice for us . . .' The rest of the conversation was taken up, chatting about Susan, and her grandfather, and Amy was smiling as she put the phone down.

Aunt Juliet was always so enthusiastic, she wore Uncle Harry out completely. It would be nice to see them again, even though it was such a sad event that had brought them all together.

Joni and Terry had married six months after Amy had left London. She had been a bridesmaid, rushing back to Cornwall as soon after the wedding as she could, terrified that she might run into Matt.

A year later they had moved out to West Germany, where Uncle Harry had arranged a job for Terry. Eighteen months later Susan had been born and now she was a beautiful little girl, with the same fair colouring as her mother.

Amy was looking forward to seeing Joni again. She missed the close friendship they had had when they lived in London. They had been good times, until Matt.

Pushing him out of her thoughts, she made an omelette for lunch, mentally listing all the things she would have to do, while she ate. She would go to the village for the extra shopping that afternoon, and then prepare a room. She jumped to her feet, after her coffee, and washed the dishes, glad to have something to occupy her mind. She needed something to think about, other than her grandfather and Matt. The news about her grandfather's accident had spread through the small community like wildfire, and a number of people stopped Amy in the village to ask about him. They all wanted to visit him, and it pleased her to know that he was so popular. She staggered back home with two laden baskets, and her arms aching.

Glancing at the clock, after storing away the shopping, and preparing the bedroom for Joni and Terry, she was amazed to find that it was nearly six o'clock. Matt would be picking her up in an hour. She felt hot and sticky, so she took a quick shower before changing, revelling in the cool, refreshing water.

She dressed in a thin brown cotton dress that

flared out elegantly from a tight bodice, and combed her lustrous hair into a neat chignon. Studying herself in the mirror, after applying mascara and lip gloss, she was surprised at her calm reflection.

The knowledge that she had lost Matt for ever had been gnawing away at her all day. Shrugging miserably, she collected a brown woollen shawl before going downstairs. She had not eaten since lunch, but she was not hungry, and she was lighting a cigarette when Matt knocked on the door. His dark eyes studied her thoroughly, his appraisal almost insolent, as he followed her into the front room. It was seven o'clock exactly. Matt was always punctual, she thought, suddenly sad at her knowledge of him. She studied him covertly as he strolled indolently towards her. Wearing a dark, formal suit that moulded his superb physique, he looked primitively male and supremely confident.

'Are you ready to leave?' The ironic gleam in his dark eyes left her in no doubt that he had seen her watching him.

'Yes, I'm ready,' she affirmed coolly, her voice polite. Ignoring the mocking smile that curved his hard mouth, she walked out to the car, leaving him to follow.

Once the car was on the main road, Matt turned his head towards her. 'Do you prefer living in Cornwall to London?' His tone was light and conversational, but Amy was not fooled. His eyes were intent and serious as they rested on her face for a brief second, before returning to the road.

She considered her reply for some time before answering, 'I prefer the country to the city,' she said carefully, noncommittally. She wondered what he was up to. They had never indulged in polite conversation, and she felt suspicious. 'Why do you ask?' Her question was spoken before she realised.

'You've lived here for three years—I wondered,' he shrugged indifferently, masking the irritation she knew he was feeling. She stared at him curiously.

'And you—do you still live in that beautiful house . . .?' She did not want to remind him of what they had once shared there. Too late. Matt glanced at her, and she knew that he was thinking about it. Unrecognisable emotion flickered for a moment in his black eyes before he turned away.

'I still own it, I don't spend much time there now—it's too big for one person.' He paused before continuing in a cool, expressionless voice. 'However, when I marry, I intend to live there permanently.'

Amy felt as though he had punched her in the stomach.

'You're getting married?' Her voice was barely above a whisper, her eyes haunted, as she stared blindly out of the window, unable to look at him.

'Yes.' His coldly spoken one-word answer struck her like another blow. The woman in his car, she supposed, and her heart ached. It should have been me, she thought miserably. She had ruined her own life, mistrusting him, and now he intended marrying someone else.

She was shaken out of her despairing apathy by the car halting in the hospital car park. Matt was speaking.

'Would you mind if I came in with you? I'd like to see him.'

Amy forced herself to speak coolly and levelly, even though she was screaming inside. 'Of course, he'll be glad to see you,' she managed, as she got out of the car.

She walked quickly towards the hospital entrance,

not wanting to be near Matt.

Her grandfather was awake as they went in, although he still looked frail and weak.

'Amy, Matt, it's good to see you together,' he smiled at them.

Amy smiled back, flushing slightly, and hoping that he would not say anything embarrassing. They pulled up chairs, and she took her grandfather's hand as they sat down.

'How are you feeling, Sam?' Matt asked gently as soon as they were seated.

'Not too bad—I can't feel a thing, they've pumped me full of drugs.' Her grandfather's reply was slow and obviously cost him a great deal of effort.

'You're looking much better, Granddad.' Amy tried to sound encouraging as she smiled warmly at him and squeezed his hand.

'I feel very tired, lass . . .' His eyes were closing even as he spoke, his shallow breathing sounding loud in the silent room.

'He keeps falling asleep,' she whispered to Matt, worry lining her face.

'It's the drugs—he'll be like this for a couple of days,' he answered reassuringly.

Amy looked at her grandfather, biting her lower lip nervously. He looked peaceful, and his breathing had steadied as he slipped into deeper sleep.

Matt stood up silently, pulling her to her feet. 'Let's go,' he mouthed, pointing to the door, and they crept out of the room carefully. Once outside, Matt turned to her.

'He'll sleep for quite a while now. I'll bring you back in the morning,' he said gently.

'No!' she answered, her voice unconsciously sharp. 'I'll get the bus.' She could not bear to see so much of him, especially knowing that he was to marry another woman.

Matt stared at her, puzzled. 'Amy, what's the matter now?'

His patience irritated her. He was treating her like a wayward child again.

'There's nothing the matter,' she retorted stiffly, childishly. 'I just don't want you to drive me here. Do you understand?'

Matt's eyes darkened ominously, his mouth thinned angrily. 'As you wish,' he said curtly, his voice cold.

They drove home in silence, each engrossed in their own thoughts. Matt's face was hard and remote, only the muscle twitching in his jaw betraying his anger.

CHAPTER TEN

Joni and Terry arrived late the next afternoon, filling the cottage with their laughter, immediately dispelling the gloomy atmosphere that seemed to have settled there since Sam Lawrence's accident.

Amy had spent a sleepless night, torturing herself with thoughts of Matt's forthcoming marriage. The thought of another woman sharing his life, secure in his love, made her bitter with jealousy. Consequently she was pale and wan, her eyes huge and bruised, like crushed petals, when they arrived.

Fortunately, Joni assumed that it was worry about her grandfather.

'You shouldn't be here on your own, Amy,' she scolded. 'I know how you worry.' Her face suddenly sobered. 'He is going to be all right, isn't he?'

'Of course he is.' Amy spoke soothingly. 'You're right, though, I do worry.' Changing the subject, she said, 'You look fantastic, Joni. I love your hair— how long have you had that style?'

Joni's pleased rejoinder changed the course of the conversation, and they chatted happily until dinner.

That Joni and Terry were supremely happy together was obvious to Amy as she watched them over the meal. She had cooked a huge steak and kidney pie, with potatoes and vegetables—'A good old-fashioned English meal,' she had laughed as she served it. They teased each other gently, their eyes warm and loving as they watched each other, and Amy sighed inwardly. How she envied them; if only Matt and she could be like that.

Joni told her all the news from Germany, her eyes shining proudly as she talked about her young daughter, promising at Amy's insistence to bring her over for Christmas. Terry watched his wife with smiling eyes, as she chattered cheerfully to Amy. He was very handsome, thought Amy, glancing at him, with his smooth sandy hair falling in a wave across his forehead, and his regular, boyish features.

The meal was unanimously enjoyed, Amy's cooking being highly praised, and Joni helped with the washing up afterwards.

'Can we go and see Granddad tonight?' she asked, drying a plate with the vigour that dictated all her actions.

'Yes, he'll be thrilled to see you,' answered Amy, smiling affectionately at her cousin.

'Is it far?'

'No, I went by bus this morning, but when Matt drives me it only takes about fifteen minutes.' Amy stopped talking, aware that Joni was staring at her open-mouthed.

'Matt?' she echoed, not taking her eyes from Amy's face.

'Yes. Matt Cavanagh,' Amy mumbled, unable to stop the hot colour that was washing up her face.

'He's here, in Cornwall?' Joni's voice was high-pitched and incredulous, her eyes still intent on Amy's lowered head.

With a great deal of effort Amy pulled herself together. 'Yes, he's renting the cottage down the lane for the summer. He's been driving me to the hospital.'

'Good heavens!'

Amy had to laugh at Joni's aghast expression.

'Don't worry, Joni. He told me yesterday that he's

getting married, so I'm quite safe.' And to her own disgust, she burst into tears.

Joni comforted her with angry eyes, and when Amy had become calmer, they sat down at the kitchen table and Joni said,

'You'd better tell me all about it. You never mentioned any of this in your letters.' She carried on, not giving Amy a chance to speak, 'My God, that man's persistent! What the hell is he doing here?'

'He said he was here on business,' Amy answered, ignoring Joni's derisive snort. 'He's divorced.'

Her cousin looked at her sympathetically. 'You still love him.' It was more of a statement than a question, and Amy nodded.

'He was at the flat, you know, that week you left, when I got back.' Amy looked up in surprise, and Joni continued, 'I know, I didn't tell you at the time, I thought it would upset you too much. I'm sorry, Amy.'

'Don't apologise, it would have upset me!' Seeing Joni's doubtful face, Amy smiled weakly, her gold eyes still full of unshed tears. 'I appreciate what you did—honestly!'

'Yes, well, when I got back from Brighton, he was outside the flat. He looked awful, weary, unshaven, and in a foul temper.' Joni paused, shuddering at her memories.

'Go on,' urged Amy, eagerly.

'He practically pushed his way into the flat. He was desperate, Amy, and I couldn't calm him down at all. He kept saying over and over again that you'd disappeared. Luckily I spotted your note before he did, and put it in my bag. I kept telling him that I didn't know what was going on, but he didn't believe me. Anyway, I made him some coffee,' she laughed reminiscently. 'I needed some myself, by then, and read your note. It was a relief to know where you were, because I was beginning to feel worried. We had coffee, and he was smoking really heavily—I can remember looking at the nicotine stains on his fingers. I didn't tell him anything, and as I'd obviously just got back, he had to believe me. In the end he left, but he made me promise to contact him if you got in touch. I felt sorry for him—he was tearing himself apart.' She gazed at Amy speculatively. 'He must have loved you, Amy, he wouldn't have behaved like that if he didn't,' she said softly.

Amy shrugged miserably. 'Well, he doesn't now, he's going to marry someone else. I didn't trust him, and now it's too late,' she sighed.

'Did you contact him when I rang you?'

Joni looked shamefaced. 'Yes, I did. I had to, he was ringing every day. I told him you were safe, but didn't want him to know where. He seemed to accept that, but an hour later he was round at the flat again. He wanted to know, and he wasn't going to give up. He obviously wasn't sleeping, and from what I could guess, drinking heavily. In the end I told him, but only after he had promised faithfully that he wouldn't contact you. I'm sorry, Amy, I've been too much of a coward to tell you this before. I didn't intend to tell him anything, after the way he had treated you, but I think he'd gone a little crazy—I couldn't let him suffer.'

Amy patted her cousin's hand.

'Don't worry, Joni, it doesn't matter anyway now!'

Joni was obviously upset, feeling that she had let Amy down, and Amy hastened to reassure her.

'I wouldn't have wanted him to suffer, honestly. I

didn't think he cared that much. You did the right thing, I promise you. I wish to God that I hadn't been so stupid—I should have let him explain . . .' she sighed; it was too late for self-recrimination. As far as Matt was concerned, it was all over. '

'How long has he been here?' Joni asked, cutting across her thoughts.

'A few weeks,' Amy replied dully. 'I thought I hated him, when he first came here,' she laughed mirthlessly, 'but that didn't last long. I nearly drowned in the bay, and he saved my life. He's so kind and gentle, and so damned attractive, I suppose I knew that I loved him all along. I tried to fight him, but I was only fighting myself. Do you understand?' She turned to Joni desperately, her eyes dull gold in her pale face.

Joni understood, Amy could see it in her face.

'We've seen each other a few times—it's inevitable in a small village like this, but these last few days he's cooled towards me, and I've been making a fool of myself. He's been polite and helpful, especially about taking me to see Granddad. Then yesterday he told me he was getting married. I've seen her, Joni, in his car, she must be staying at the cottage. It hurt so much, I keep thinking that it should be me. I need to get away, I can't stand to see them together—I'm sorry to burden you with all my troubles . . .' Amy could not speak; her throat was closing up, tears soaking her face.

Joni put her arms around Amy, angry with Matt Cavanagh. How could he flaunt his future wife in front of Amy? Was this some sort of twisted revenge? She held Amy tightly, letting her cry, hoping she would feel better for it. Amy cried until she had no more tears left and she was a dry, empty husk.

'I'm sorry, Joni,' she whispered, wiping her face.

Another apology.

'Listen, Amy, I've had an idea,' said Joni. 'Are you serious about getting away?' Amy nodded wordlessly. 'Because if you are, why don't you come back to Germany with us? I know that Terry's firm is always in need of good secretaries, and you could pick up the language easily.' Her eyes were shining hopefully, as she stared at Amy.

'I couldn't leave Granddad,' Amy answered dully, not really taking in what Joni was saying.

'We could sort something out—do say you'll think about it, Amy. From what you've said about Matt, it's over between you two. Start a new life, and try to forget him.' Joni was persuasive and enthusiastic.

'I'll never forget him,' Amy muttered sadly. 'But I do appreciate what you're trying to do, Joni, and I will think about it, I promise,' she smiled wanly. 'We'd better be getting back to Terry, he'll wonder what on earth we're doing in here! I'll go and change, then we'll go and see Granddad, shall we?'

'Right.' Joni stood up, her eyes worried as they rested on her cousin, realising that she could do no more.

'Thanks, Joni, I needed someone to talk to,' said Amy, then slipped upstairs to shower and change. Her mind was racing as she stepped into the shower. The possibility of moving to Germany was attractive. Apart from her grandfather, and a few friends, there was nothing to keep her in England. Joni and the rest of her family were in Germany. She would consider it, as she had promised Joni.

She dressed quickly, eager to see her grandfather, in a violet cotton skirt with an embroidered waistband, that fell in soft folds around her slender legs, and a tee-shirt, in a lighter shade of mauve. She clipped back her hair with two tortoiseshell combs, leaving it to hang down her back, soft and loose, and applied some make-up. Looking at herself in the mirror as she stroked mascara on to her thick lashes, she felt miserable. She really would have to get a good night's sleep—she looked dreadful! She was unaware that the hollows and shadows in her face gave her a haunting, mysterious beauty of great depth.

Throwing down the mascara and sighing discontentedly, she ran downstairs to join the others.

Terry had hired a car for the duration of their stay in England, and they drove to the hospital, with Amy giving directions. As they walked along the corridor to Sam Lawrence's room, Matt suddenly appeared round the corner. Filled with dismay, Amy felt her heart beat faster at the sight of him, in tight denim jeans and a dark shirt. He walked gracefully towards them, a slight smile curving his hard mouth, as Amy stammered her greeting.

'H—Hello, Matt. Have you been to see Granddad?'

'I have indeed,' he replied coolly, his dark eyes intent as he stared at her, taking in the paleness of her face, and the dark shadows beneath her haunted golden eyes. 'He's much better tonight.' His gaze flicked over Joni and Terry, standing just behind Amy, and she realised that she had not introduced them.

'Matt, you know Joni, my cousin, and Terry Seymour, her husband. Terry, Matt Cavanagh.'

Matt and Terry shook hands, and Matt smiled dazzlingly at Joni, who managed a tight-lipped grin in response.

'Are you staying in England long?' Matt asked them smoothly. He was using his charm, Amy thought disgustedly.

'About a week,' Joni replied, smiling prettily now.

Watching her, Amy could see that she was not immune to Matt's charm. He really was a most extraordinary man. She knew that Joni was angry with him, but could not help herself responding to Matt's totally male, charismatic personality.

Bringing her attention back to the conversation, she listened to them chatting about Cornwall. Amazed, she saw that Joni was smiling up into Matt's face now, and Terry was listening to him intently, an expression of respect on his face.

'Will you be going to the Midsummer Dance this weekend?' Matt's darkly charming glance slid to Amy as he spoke.

'A dance?' Joni clapped her hands, clearly delighted at the prospect. 'Oh yes! Can we go, love?' Her eyes pleaded to Terry.

'Of course,' Terry answered, laughing.

'You never told us about this, Amy!' Joni mock-scolded her.

'I'd forgotten all about it,' admitted Amy honestly. 'Of course we'll go.'

'Will you be going, Matt?' Joni looked up into his face, her eyes still smiling.

He nodded, grinning indulgently at her. 'Yes, I believe it's a big event in the social calendar.' His eyes flicked back to Amy, who was thinking, now I know that he's going, I certainly won't be. 'I'll see you there, then.'

Amy knew that he was talking to her, and managed a bland smile.

'Yes, and you must introduce us to your fiancée,' she murmured, her voice brittle, and her eyes flashing anger at him, satisfied to see his momentary impatience with her insolence.

'Amy told me that you're getting married. What's

she like?' Joni cut across the tension between them, candid interest in her expression.

Still looking at Amy, Matt replied softly, 'She's beautiful,' a mocking smile curving his lips as he spoke.

Pain slashed through Amy at the gentle reverence in his voice. She felt like cutting his throat as she turned away, suddenly impatient to be away from him.

Noticing her withdrawal, Matt politely said goodbye to Joni and Terry, then turning to Amy said, 'I'll see you on Saturday, Amy.'

She nodded without looking up, reluctant to let him see the pain in her eyes.

He strolled away indolently, and she watched him from under her eyelashes, unable to tear her hungry glance away from his powerful body and feline grace of movement.

Joni too, was watching him. 'Phew, what a man!' she giggled. 'He's only got to look at me, and I go weak at the knees!'

'Hey, remember me?' Terry laughed good-naturedly, taking her arm and propelling her down the corridor.

Amy followed, smiling at their gentle teasing, but inside she felt sick. She had committed herself to attending the Midsummer Dance, not expecting Matt to be there. Perhaps she could cry off with a headache—no, that would not work, because she knew that Joni and Terry would not go without her, and she would not spoil their brief stay in England.

It seemed as though she would have to go, and bear the pain and humiliation of seeing Matt and his future wife together, with a smile. Would she never be free of him? As they walked into her grandfather's room, she decided to think seriously about

Joni's suggestion of going back to Germany with them. It would mean running away again, but at that moment she did not care.

Her grandfather was dozing, but woke up at the sound of them entering the room.

'Granddad, look who's here!' Amy exclaimed excitedly as she kissed him.

'Joni and Terry! I can hardly believe it, come in and sit down.' Sam Lawrence was thrilled to see them, his eyes bright with joy. 'You've just missed Matt,' he said to Amy.

'I know, we met him on the way out.' Amy hoped that nobody had noticed her blushing face as she spoke.

Fortunately, the conversation turned back to her grandfather, as Joni and Terry started asking about the accident. Amy listened absently, unable to shake Matt's image out of her mind. She smiled and nodded, but her attention was elsewhere.

Her grandfather was still very weak, and she could tell by his glazed eyes that he was still heavily drugged. After ten minutes, the strain of keeping his eyes open proved too much, and he slipped easily into sleep.

Joni looked across at Amy, her eyes full of worried questions. Amy explained in low, whispering tones.

'They've filled him full of drugs for the pain, and they make him fall asleep very easily. We'd better go now.'

They moved quietly out of the room. In the corridor Joni began to cry, turning to Terry instinctively and burying her head against his shoulder.

'He looks so old and weak,' she sniffed, her face distraught. 'He's not going to die, is he?' She lifted her head and stared at Amy wildly.

'No, he's not going to die, he's doing very well.

You must remember that he's getting on, and a broken limb is always more serious in an older person. It just takes longer, that's all.' Amy took Joni's hand and squeezed it comfortingly. 'I wouldn't tell you lies Joni, honestly.'

Joni dried her eyes, reassured by the quiet sincerity in Amy's voice. Terry slipped his arm round her shoulders, and they all left the hospital, walking slowly to the car.

They drove home in silence. Amy was terribly worried about her grandfather. The nurse always spoke encouragingly about his progress and there was no reason to imagine that the hospital staff would lie—nevertheless, she could not help being suspicious. He did look very ill.

On reaching home, Amy made coffee for them and they sat around in easy chairs, drinking the fresh aromatic beverage and chatting. There seemed to Amy's overwrought imagination to be a curiously strained atmosphere. She knew that she was over-tired, confused and worried, so she excused herself early and took a warm relaxing bath, luxuriating in the perfumed softness of the water until she knew that she would sleep.

The week flew past, with the Midsummer Dance looming ominously at the end of it for Amy. It was strange how dreaded events came so quickly, she mused, while longed-for events took forever to arrive. They would all visit her grandfather twice a day, and the rest of their time was packed to the full. They sunbathed and swam in Amy's private cove, and walked for miles in the surrounding countryside, taking picnics, and usually getting lost.

They drove to London for a day's shopping, with Amy feeling absurdly safe, knowing that Matt was in Cornwall. He had an uncanny knack of turning up when she was least expecting to see him. Amy had not visited London for some years, and it was good to walk round the shops again. She was depressingly resigned to going to the dance, and with this in mind bought an evening dress. Joni had already bought her dress, a scarlet embroidered caftan that suited her perfectly, complementing her fair colouring and adding a bright sparkle to her blue eyes.

After a good deal of laughing indecision Amy chose a deep brown velvet dress, with a low neckline and long sleeves. The rich colour darkened her gold eyes to a mysterious burnished honey colour, and added lustre to her dark hair. The simple, clinging style hinted at the smooth rounded curves beneath, and Amy knew that she looked her best in it. She would need to, because the thought of another encounter with Matt filled her with dread as well as longing.

Joni bought more clothes, complaining loudly about the shops in Germany, in an effort to appease Terry, who was not particularly fond of shopping, and was teasing Joni about her extravagant expenditure.

The day was a huge success, and they drove back to Cornwall with aching feet, tired but content.

The Thursday before the dance Terry took both girls for a meal at a recently opened restaurant outside Falmouth. The intimate atmosphere made it popular, and the food was highly recommended. They were shown to their table by a deferential waiter, who hovered about silently, taking their orders. Glancing round, when he had gone, Amy approved of the rich wood panelling that gave the place an intimate warmth. Most of the diners were couples, some of them so engrossed in each other that they could not possibly be aware of what they were eating. Remembering her intimate dinners with Matt, Amy smiled sadly. How she missed him!

She had just finished her delicious, tender steak, when she felt someone's eyes upon her. The feeling of being watched was so strong that she shivered involuntarily, turning her head to see who it was, and her stomach somersaulted as her glance collided with Matt. Sitting to her left, at the other side of the room, he lifted his glass to her in a silent, mocking salute, sardonic amusement in his black eyes.

Amy turned away immediately, her heart beating painfully fast, and smoothed her damp palms over the black silk of her tunic. Glancing through her eyelashes, she studied his companion surreptitiously. It was the woman she had seen in his car—his fiancée. She was very attractive, her dark hair styled fashionably, and the tailored white suit that she was wearing gave her an exotic look. Amy felt bitterly jealous as she watched the woman smiling and laughing softly with Matt, who was giving her his undivided, charming attention. Suddenly the restaurant was a trap that she could not escape from. She forced herself to eat and talk normally, but all her senses were directed towards the other side of the room. She was singularly aware of him, every languid, graceful movement that he made, without looking at him.

As she sipped her coffee she could feel his enigmatic eyes upon her, and she gripped the cup tighter, finding it almost impossible to carry on normally with those dark eyes focused so intently in her direction.

Finally Terry suggested that they leave, and Amy jumped to her feet, sighing with relief, wishing that she had had the courage to leave thirty minutes earlier. She smoothed back her sleek hair nervously, aware of Matt's dark glance travelling over her slowly, as she made her way out of the restaurant at a determinedly slow pace.

Once outside, she felt dazed with relief that he had not come over to their table, as she pressed her hand to the thundering pulse in her throat. She had got out of the restaurant unscathed, unspoken to, and she felt absurdly free as they strolled towards the car. She would have to exercise more control at the dance, she thought miserably, disgusted with the almost overpowering urge that had nearly sent her running from her table a few minutes before . . .

The next morning, feeling decisive, she rang Howard. He was pleased to hear from her, and her heart sank when he asked her to accompany him to the Midsummer Dance. It was so very tempting to accept just to get back at Matt. However, her honesty prevailed and she refused. She also quietly explained about Matt and her love for him. It was humiliating, but Howard deserved to know. She got the feeling that he had already guessed, but had said nothing. Amy knew that he was hurt, and longed to be able to comfort him in some way. She apologised for being so cowardly and not telling him face to face, and was grateful for his understanding. Howard asked about her grandfather, and by the time Amy put down the receiver, she had tears in her eyes. How could he be so kind when she had hurt him so? How she wished that Matt Cavanagh meant nothing to her!

CHAPTER ELEVEN

As she shampooed her dark hair, Amy felt an unusual feeling of apprehension building up inside her, as she contemplated the evening ahead. The thought of seeing Matt again stirred her deepest senses, even as she dreaded it. Sighing, she rinsed her hair and stepped out of the shower.

She dried her hair carefully and reached for the filmy underwear that was strewn across the bed. Wrapping herself in a silk robe, she examined her face critically as she began to apply her make-up. Her thoughts were fatalistic as she stroked her eyelids with light, honey-coloured shadow. She could not bear to go on seeing Matt; it was tearing her apart, meeting him accidentally, around the village with his fiancée.

She had not slept after the incident in the restaurant on Thursday, and the following night had been filled with nightmares. She was suffering, and it showed in her face, she thought miserably as she applied mascara.

She made up carefully, finishing with pale lip lustre, and standing back from the mirror saw that she had managed to disguise perfectly the ravages of the past week. She looked good, and she needed the confidence that this knowledge gave her, if she was to face Matt Cavanagh with dignity.

She coiled her heavy swathe of hair into an elegant loop on the top of her head and pinned it with an elaborate gold comb that had belonged to her grandmother. A few carefully casual strands caressed her smooth cheeks and the nape of her neck; the effect was cool and chic, and she was pleased with the fragile look it gave her.

She slid into her velvet gown, the sleek material sensuously cool against her warm skin. It fitted her perfectly, and a satisfied smile curved her soft mouth as she hung large gold hoops on her ears. She looked beautiful. She would show Matt Cavanagh that she did not give a damn who he married.

The final touch before she left her bedroom to join Joni and Terry downstairs was to dab the haunting floral perfume that she always wore behind her ears, and on other pulse spots.

She was first to be ready—probably in her eagerness to get the evening over with, she thought wryly, as she stared at the tray of drinks on the sideboard. She did not drink spirit as a rule, but tonight she needed it.

She poured herself a small measure of gin, wrinkling her nose distastefully at the smell, and added orange juice, hoping it would take some of the raw taste away. She was sipping it slowly as Joni came into the room.

'You've started early,' she laughed, eyeing the glass in Amy's hand curiously.

'I'm just getting into a party mood,' Amy answered, taking another gulp of the gin and feeling it affecting her immediately.

She did not have to explain to Joni; her cousin knew the apprehension she was feeling at seeing Matt again.

The red caftan looked stunning, and Amy remarked on it.

'You look gorgeous, that dress is perfect for you,' she said honestly.

Joni twirled round, pleased at the compliment.

'Yes, I love it.' She studied Amy's appearance in return. 'And you look beautiful, Amy, really lovely.'

'I don't want to go.' Amy's blurted confession surprised herself. 'I can't stand seeing them together!'

Joni took her arm, and poured out another two gins and orange, sticking one into Amy's hand.

'You'll be with Terry and me. You'll be okay—just show him that you don't give a damn, ignore him—anything, but don't run away. You did it on Thursday, and you can do it again.' Noticing Amy's look of surprise, she explained, 'Oh yes, I saw him in the restaurant, staring at you. You coped admirably. Honestly, Amy, you were cool and dignified.'

The doubt on Amy's face was obvious. 'I wanted to run out of the restaurant,' she admitted ruefully. 'But you're right, I've got to prove to myself that I can do it.' She swallowed the last of her drink, and the alcohol went straight to her head, filling her with Dutch courage. 'Just stick by me, Joni,' she pleaded.

'I will, love,' Joni promised.

Terry came downstairs, looking formal and very handsome, in a dark grey suit, and looked at both girls appreciatively.

'Lucky me,' he remarked smilingly, 'accompanying the two most beautiful women in the village.' Laughing at his extravagant compliments, they left the cottage and made their way down to the village hall.

The Midsummer Dance was held every year in the village hall. Everybody dressed up, and enjoyed themselves tremendously. The hall was festooned with streamers and fairy lights that glowed brightly on the dancing couples. A bar was set up, and long trestle tables at one end of the room groaned under the weight of the mouthwatering buffet, contributions to which were sent by everyone in the village.

There was always something magical about this one night of the year, and many a romance had blossomed under the bewitching coloured lights, to the strains of sweet music. Joni and Amy glanced round with interest, as Terry made his way to the bar.

'It's enchanting,' breathed Joni, with sparkling eyes. 'The atmosphere is incredible!'

'I know, at any other time, it's just an ordinary hall, but on this one night every year, it's almost as if a spell has been cast, and everything changes,' Amy answered, unconsciously scanning the hall for the tall, broad-shouldered figure who would almost certainly ruin her evening. She could not see him— maybe he would not come after all.

She could also see no sign of Howard, and she realised that she had ruined his evening. He would not come knowing that she was here.

She had seen him once since she had telephoned him, a chance meeting in the village. He had been closed and distant, though as polite as ever. He knew, as she did, what it was like to love and not have that love returned, and she was miserable at the loss of his friendship. But with her misery came relief; at least she could not hurt him again.

Her worried thoughts were interrupted by a tall, fair young man with a boyish face and a strangely sweet smile, who asked her to dance. Amy knew him as a worker on a local farm and smiling her acceptance, took his arm as he led her on to the dance floor. They moved slowly to the soft music. Amy was a good dancer, having been taught by her grandfather, and the young man, whose name was Tom, was enchanted by her, as she smiled up into his face. He was very young and tonguetied, so they did not talk much, and Amy gave herself up to the gentle rhythm of the dance.

The music had just stopped, and Tom was leading her back to Joni and Terry, when her eyes fell upon Matt, as he entered the hall with his fiancée. He was looking at Amy, and the deep awareness that she always felt when she saw him made her heart pound, as she broke the eye-contact between them. He was looking big and disturbing in a light linen suit, that moulded the powerful width of his broad shoulders and muscular chest. His companion was wearing a cream lace dress that suited her dark colouring. She looked stunning, thought Amy wearily, wishing that she was dead. They made their way over to the bar, and Amy's eyes followed them intently. Matt's strong hand was curved lightly, possessively, at his fiancée's elbow, and he was leaning towards her, making her smile as he talked.

Amy turned away, feeling sick, to find Joni watching her sympathetically. 'I'm fine,' she lied reassuringly, finishing her drink in one mouthful, and any further conversation between the two girls was cut short by another young man claiming Amy for a dance. She accepted readily, needing something to do other than watch Matt and his partner, who were just stepping on to the dance floor themselves.

She could feel Matt's eyes upon her, and not daring to look up, she knew that his expression would be coolly mocking, as the two couples passed each other. Consequently she smiled up at her partner alluringly, sliding her hands along his shoulders and flirting unashamedly. Her languid inviting gaze met Matt's and, satisfied, she watched his eyes narrow coldly with anger at her obvious behaviour. Her smile widened as her glance skittered to his tightly-compressed mouth. His irritation was obvious, and for a moment Amy felt sorry for his companion, blissfully unaware of the tension that was stretching between Matt and herself. Then she was smoothly swung away, and Matt was lost to view. The evening passed quickly. Amy, intoxicated by her power to annoy Matt, danced with a number of eager young men, her reckless mood attracting them like bees round a honeypot. She sparkled brilliantly, her shining gold eyes inviting even as they rebuked. A number of times during the evening she felt Matt's cold angry eyes on her, and the thought of his frustration exhilarated her. He had no hold over her—she was as free as a bird, and he knew it, she thought, amused.

She sat down to eat with Joni and Terry. The food was delicious, but she hardly tasted it, her eyes still on Matt, who was leaning indolently against the bar. There was no sign of his fiancée. Perhaps she had left early, unwilling to put up with Matt's foul temper. It would serve him right, Amy thought nastily.

They still had not spoken a word to each other, and Amy felt that it was almost too good to be true. And then Matt made his move.

Amy was dancing with Tom, whose admiring eyes could not be torn away from her brightly beautiful face, when Matt cut in. His eyes were dangerous, his stance threatening, as he tapped Tom's shoulder, and the younger man reacted immediately. Amy said nothing as Matt's arms went around her, but her heart was racing away. She leaned against him, feeling his body tighten as she touched him, and laughed out loud. As they moved slowly together, she realised that she had wanted this all night. 'What the hell do you think you're playing at?' he muttered softly, for her ears alone.

'What do you mean?' Amy smiled up at him innocently, glimmering invitation in her eyes, and her softly parted lips.

'You know damn well what I mean—flirting with every man in the room. You need a good slap!' His dark eyes were glinting fire between the heavy narrowed lids.

'And am I going to get it from you?' she asked, sweetly insolent. 'I'm sure your fiancée wouldn't approve.'

He stared at her intently. 'Are you drunk?' he grated.

She laughed, light, tinkling laughter. 'I might be, I don't know. You tell me,' she murmured provocatively. She knew that she was playing a dangerous game, but she did not care. Matt's nearness was going to her head like wine, and he could not touch her in front of all these people.

'You're asking for trouble, Amy. Is that what you want?' His temper was barely controlled now, his voice low, as he stared down at her. Ignoring his question, she let her hand slide over his shoulder, to tangle in the thick black hair that touched his collar. She heard his indrawn breath at her caress, and his hard arms tightened around her as they moved perfectly across the dance floor.

Amy pressed the seductive length of her body against his, uncaring in that moment of madness that he was engaged to somebody else. Her movements supple, she slid her thigh against the hardness of his, feeling the pulsing heat inside her, and gazed into his strong face, her eyes mysterious pools of magic.

'You need some air,' Matt muttered harshly, moving her towards the door. 'You little fool, stay off the drink in future!'

'You're not my keeper, Matt,' she laughed as he propelled her into the warm night air, his grip on the soft flesh of her upper arm painfully tight.

'No?' His question was cold and angry, and filled with a wealth of meaning that she could not understand.

They walked into the garden behind the hall. The air was sweetly-scented and quiet, and Amy walked slowly over the grass, kicking off her shoes as she went, revelling in the soft coolness beneath her bare feet.

The moon was almost full, filling the garden with a gentle silver light, and she breathed in deeply, suddenly glad to be away from the bright noise and heat of the dance. She was not drunk, and the realisation that they were alone in the quiet garden worried her. Matt was just behind her, and she turned towards him quickly, suspiciously, noticing how big and almost threatening he looked in the dim light.

He was staring at her, his eyes still dark with anger, as they rested intently on her upturned face.

Irritated, she suspected him of tricking her into coming out here alone with him, and turned away from him, her gaze scanning the dark garden, and the gentle hills beyond. The scene before her was heartbreakingly familiar.

'I'll miss it so much if I go,' she murmured, almost to herself, and felt Matt stiffen behind her.

'What do you mean?' He was still, his voice carefully controlled and low, as she held his attention.

Amy suddenly felt reckless again. She wanted to shock him, to show him that he did not matter to her any more.

'I'm going back to Germany with Joni and Terry,

they can get me a job there,' she lied defiantly,
without looking at him.

'*No!*' Matt's denial was torn out of him, savage
and furious.

She spun round to face him angrily. His face was
pale and twisted, his glittering eyes bleak and tor-
mented. She stared at him, wondering if he was ill.

'You can't stop me, Matt,' she whispered, feeling
frightened.

'I can and I will,' he hissed furiously. 'I won't let
you go again, Amy. I can't let you go—I love you!'

His words left her breathless as she gazed up into
his face.

'Y . . . you love me . . .?' she faltered weakly,
unable to believe it.

'Yes!' His voice was still angry and tortured. 'God,
how I love you!'

She was still staring at him, still doubting the
words that she had been waiting so many years to
hear, when his control snapped and he reached for
her savagely, pulling her into the hard warmth of
his arms, and opening her mouth hungrily with his
own. His mouth was fierce and urgent with the
agony of their long separation.

Amy clung to him, her head spinning, responding
fully to his passionate demands, pulling his head
down to hers, when he would have released her, and
kissing him desperately. His arms tightened around
her, his kiss deep and demanding, and his powerful
body urgent with passion and love, at last admitted.

Finally Matt lifted his dark head and gazed at
her with glittering eyes, his face still pale. 'I can't let
you go, my love,' he repeated softly. 'I need you,
you complete me, and you're going to marry me
whether you like it or not.'

'But, Matt, your fiancée...' Amy's voice trailed off, as he began to laugh.

'What's so funny?' she asked with irritation, punching him lightly, jealousy flashing in her gold eyes.

'Louise is my secretary—hired on your suggestion, sweet Amy, don't you remember? You wouldn't do the job, so I hired her.' He grinned at the confusion in her face, and pulled her closer against him, unable to repress his need for her. 'When I told you that I intended to marry, I meant you, foolish child.' He touched her cheek gently. 'When we met in the hospital, I realised that you'd misunderstood, and thought I'd meant Louise. So I took her out a couple of times, hoping it would make you jealous,' he smiled unashamedly.

'Well, it did,' she admitted freely. 'But didn't...?'

'I told her all about you, she agreed to help me—anyway, she's a happily engaged lady,' Matt answered, reading her mind, as he claimed her lips once more.

Desire flared up between them, burning them both, as they clung together, straining closer, in mutual need. Pulling away suddenly, Amy needed to know something.

'How long have you loved me?' she asked guilelessly, sliding her hands beneath his shirt to the hair-coarsened skin below, delighting in his immediate response.

Matt smiled down at her. 'Since the moment I first saw you,' he answered honestly. 'I walked into the gallery, and it hit me like a ton of bricks. You were so beautiful, in that yellow dress, so innocent, I had to have you. As I got to know you better, I realised that I wanted to marry you, but I wasn't free.' He kissed her forehead with gentle lips. 'You were very young, and I was thirty—too old for you, and I had to hold myself back all the time for fear of frightening you away.'

Amy lifted her shoulders sadly, remembering his cool withdrawal. 'I could hardly bear your rejection,' she murmured shyly.

'I never meant to hurt you, Amy. When you came to me, that day in my studio——' he shook his head as he spoke, 'my God, you were lovely! I'm not a saint, I wanted you. Even when I found out that you were—well, untouched, I couldn't keep my hands off you, even though I'd promised myself that I wouldn't touch you until we were married.'

Amy was sliding her hands caressingly over his body, as he spoke, and he groaned as she touched him.

'You never told me that you loved me,' she said, pressing her lips to his strong throat.

'Every time I looked at you, every time I touched you, I was shouting it with my heart and my body. I thought it was obvious—words seemed unimportant,' he answered sadly, his eyes sincere on her face.

Thinking back, Amy remembered his gentle passion, the reverence of his touch and the love in his eyes, that she had been too young and too stupid to recognise.

Matt continued, needing to set things straight between them. 'Then that bitch Celine poisoned you against me. It hurt and angered me that you didn't trust me, that you believed her, and I forced myself on you that last night. I needed to show you that what she'd said was untrue, that there was only you, but it all went wrong—I frightened you away, and I felt an utter swine.' His eyes were haunted as he remembered. 'I wanted to get down on my knees and beg you to forgive me, but you'd gone, and I went crazy.'

'Matt, I'm so sorry,' Amy whispered, shaken by his misery. 'I did believe Celine, I'll never forgive myself for that. I had no confidence in myself, and I loved you too much, and I had to get away. You'd never said that you loved me, and I couldn't bear to be just your mistress, because I wanted to live with you, share your life, have your children . . .' She broke off, blushing furiously.

Matt tilted up her downturned face, his eyes dark and intent. 'You will have my children,' he promised huskily, his expression making her feel weak inside. 'Soon.' This last murmured word was devastating in its sincere promise, and Amy swallowed convulsively.

'But you didn't follow me down here, we didn't meet again for three years,' she complained teasingly.

'I thought I'd killed any love you had for me after that night— anyway, I was in a pretty bad way for at least a year after you left—drinking heavily.' He smiled ruefully, running his hand wearily around his neck. 'I tried to get over you, I went abroad for a couple of years—trying to forget. But in the end I had to find out if I could free myself, by seeing you again. I expected you to be married, and I thought I could exorcise your ghost by seeing you with your husband, and maybe children.' He shrugged gracefully. 'But when I saw you again I knew that I'd been kidding myself—I loved you more than I could have imagined, and if you had been married I think I would have killed your husband. As it was I could hardly keep my hands off Jordan. Does that frighten you?'

Amy smiled up at him brilliantly. 'It doesn't

frighten me, it thrills me. I love you, Matt, I've never stopped loving you, and the power of your love reassures me, protects me . . .'

She was silenced by his mouth, hungry and insistent. She knew that he was shaken by her admission of love, and she gave herself up completely to the ecstasy of his embrace. After long minutes of silence he put her away from him firmly, and continued explaining.

'I thought I'd try to win you back slowly. I met your grandfather in the village, and had a long talk with him. He approved of what I was trying to do.' He stopped, seeing Amy's astounded face.

She laughed. 'The sly old thing! He never told me anything about it.'

'Ah well, that's because I swore him to secrecy, and persuaded him to ask me to dinner. Don't blame him, my love. I can be very persuasive when I choose to be.'

'I know,' she murmured invitingly, wrapping her arms around his neck.

'Anyway, it didn't work, you seemed totally uninterested, and I found myself losing my temper all the time, but I still couldn't keep away from you. The night you asked me to stay—I couldn't take advantage of you. You were miserable and lonely, and I had to force myself to walk away—I felt sure that you would have regretted it. But I'm telling you now, Amy, you're not going to Germany. I've waited too long for you, and you're going to marry me—tomorrow if possible,' he finished decisively, his dark eyes disturbing as they rested on her mouth.

'I'll marry you tonight if you want, dear Matt. I love you.' Her arms tightened around his neck, as he possessed her mouth once more, his hands sliding slowly over her body, leaving her in no doubt about his feelings.

'Just one more question, Matt,' she whispered, as his lips moved to her throat, sending shivers of excitement through her.

He lifted his head reluctantly, and her heart pounded at the expression in his eyes.

'Did you finish that painting of me?'

He took her hand. 'Come, I'll show you.' He led her to his car and she got in, puzzled.

'What . . .?' she began.

'Wait and see,' he smiled at her.

They drove up to his cottage, Amy watching him with curiosity in her gold eyes. How good it was to be able to watch him openly.

Matt drove in silence, a slight smile curving his hard mouth. As soon as they arrived he took her hand and led her inside and upstairs. Once inside his bedroom, she gasped, realising why he had brought her there. All around the room hung paintings of her in the gold dress. She was beautiful, painted with love. Matt was watching her as she gazed around. There were at least fifteen paintings created from his memory, and they laid bare his heart, if she had any doubt about his love for her.

She turned to him, tears welling up in her eyes. He was holding the dress, the golden dream dress in his hands.

'It's yours,' he said softly, echoing the past. 'A gift of love. I bought it when I was little more than a child myself. It seemed to me then that when I found the woman it belonged to, she would be mine, for ever.' He shrugged. 'A young boy's dream, but it's true.'

Amy could not speak as he handed her the dress. All her fear and loneliness was gone, and her future was full of promise and hope with the man she loved.

Matt cupped her face with strong, gentle hands. 'I love you, Amy,' he said simply. 'I'll love you for ever.'

And the world was in his dark eyes as he bent his head.

Harlequin Plus

THE BEAUTY OF CRETE

The most southerly and the largest of the Greek islands,
Crete leaves her visitors with images of rugged mountains,
of astoundingly beautiful gorges, of plains rich with
vegetation, and of a turquoise sea dashing fiercely on the
rocks or lapping gently at sandy beaches.

Most of the island's hotels are on the north coast. The
leading resort town, Agios Nikolaos, toward the east, is a
pleasant port backed by a dramatic cliff-enclosed
salt-water lake. Hania, toward the west, has a dual charm.
The old quarter, surrounding the port, is graced by narrow
lanes and dominated by Venetian fortresses. Above it
stretches the modern town with attractive houses set
among handsome gardens.

It was in Crete 4,500 years ago that the first European
civilization, that of the Minoans, was born. Today in the
ruins of Knossos, visitors tour the mazes of Minoan
palaces where frescoes show the high level of this ancient
culture. The passage of later civilizations is reflected
elsewhere, in the island's Venetian castles and Byzantine
churches.

Crete is an island of beautiful and fascinating places—
but even more, Crete is people . . . where a visitor can
happen upon a party in progress or join a local festival,
listen to the men play the lira, sing folk songs and tell of
the proud and noble history of their island.

SUPERROMANCE

Longer, exciting, sensual and dramatic!

Fascinating love stories that will hold
you in their magical spell till the last page
is turned!

Now's your chance to discover the earlier
books in this exciting series. Choose from
the great selection on the following page!

Choose from this list of great
SUPERROMANCES!